MOONLIGHT ORIGINS
THE MAKING OF A WEREWOLF DETECTIVE

THE ETHAN REEVES WEREWOLF DETECTIVE SERIES
BOOK FOUR

RAE STONEHOUSE

LIVE FOR EXCELLENCE PRODUCTIONS

PROLOGUE: NIGHT OF THE FIRST CHANGE

The full moon hung like a spotlight in the October sky as Detective Ethan Reeves chased the suspect down Harper Street. His lungs burned, but something else burned deeper - an unfamiliar fire in his blood that had been building all day. Sweat drenched his shirt despite the autumn chill.

"Police! Stop!" His voice came out as more growl than command, startling even him.

The suspect darted into Oakwood Cemetery, weaving between weathered headstones. Ethan followed, but his vision kept blurring, shifting between crystal clarity and strange colors he'd never seen before. The world seemed to pulse with new smells - wet earth, rotting leaves, old stone, and something metallic that made his stomach turn.

His bones ached like they were trying to reshape themselves. This wasn't normal exhaustion. This was something else, something that traced back to that bizarre attack three weeks ago. The doctors had found no infection, and said the wounds healed unusually fast. Too fast.

The suspect scaled the cemetery's back wall. Ethan moved to follow, but a shaft of moonlight hit him directly. The burning erupted into white-hot agony. He dropped to his knees, watching in horror as his fingers began to elongate.

His jaw cracked and extended, teeth sharpening into points as fur erupted across his skin. The pain was excruciating, but worse was the hunger - a primal, ravening thing clawing its way up from deep inside. His senses exploded with information: the rapid heartbeat of a rabbit hiding in the bushes fifty yards away, the lingering scent of cigarette smoke from a groundskeeper's break hours ago, the whisper of cars on the highway two miles distant.

Through the haze of transformation, he saw movement at the top of the cemetery wall. The suspect - no, not suspect, he realized as his enhanced vision cut through the darkness. Hunter. The figure perched there watching him, lips curled in a predatory smile that revealed gleaming fangs.

"Welcome to the pack, Detective Reeves," the hunter said, voice carrying easily to Ethan's newly sensitive ears." We've been waiting for you."

Then the hunter was gone, leaving Ethan alone with the moon, the night, and the terrifying knowledge that everything he thought he knew about his city's dark underbelly was just the surface of a much deeper, more dangerous reality.

His police radio crackled with his partner's voice, searching for him. But he couldn't answer anymore. Not like this. Never again as just a normal detective.

The change took him completely then, and Detective Ethan Reeves vanished into the shadows of Oakwood Cemetery, replaced by something that howled at the moon and ran with four legs instead of two.

The hunt was on, but he wasn't sure anymore who was the hunter and who was the prey.

COPYRIGHT

Published by Live For Excellence Productions

ISBN:

Ebook: 978-1-998591-43-5

Paperback: 978-1-998591-44-2

Audiobook: 978-1-998591-45-9

PART ONE: FRAGMENTS OF THE PAST

CHAPTER ONE

THE CHANGE

Detective Ethan Reeves crouched beside the body in Daybridge's industrial district, the acrid smell of rust and river water mixing with something darker - something his enhanced senses now recognized as supernatural violence. Three parallel gashes carved across the victim's torso told a story his old self would have dismissed as impossible. His hands trembled as he documented the scene, each camera flash threatening to trigger the transformation building under his skin.

The midnight air hummed with unseen energies, every shadow concealing potential threats his newfound instincts screamed to confront. The moon, three-quarters full, pulled at his bones like an invisible tide. Even the gentle October breeze carried information his human mind struggled to process - territorial markers, supernatural signatures, the lingering traces of violence beyond mortal understanding.

"You should have come to us sooner," a voice spoke softly behind him. Dana Walker emerged from the darkness with fluid grace, her movements betraying inhuman precision. Her official title - "Supernatural Community Liaison" - appeared on city paperwork, but Ethan now knew it masked a much older role. She was a bridge between worlds, maintaining ancient balances while navigating modern bureaucracy.

Ethan straightened, fighting another wave of pre-transformation pain. "Didn't exactly know who to trust," he managed, his voice rough with suppressed change. "Hard to find werewolves in the phone book."

Dana's expression softened with centuries of accumulated wisdom. "You're not the first detective to walk this path. During the Great Depression, Detective James Morrison faced the same challenge. He was turned during the Harbor District riots - officially labeled as labor disputes, but actually a supernatural territorial war."

She moved closer, her presence somehow steadying the chaos in his shifting body. "Morrison helped establish the first formal agreement between Daybridge law enforcement and our world. The Morrison Accords of 1934 created structure where there was only shadow, gave rules to ancient powers that had operated unchecked."

Ethan's world tilted as another transformation wave hit. Dana caught his arm, her supernatural strength keeping him upright. The crime scene lights blurred and sharpened rhythmically as his vision fluctuated between human and wolf.

"The Accords weren't just about law enforcement," Dana continued, her voice anchoring him to reality. "After the Blood Wars of 1897, when the Crimson Court tried to claim Daybridge as vampire territory, Morrison's pack established a new balance. Every supernatural faction gained representation, but werewolves became the city's protectors - guardians of both human law and supernatural order."

Memories of three weeks ago crashed through Ethan's mind: Following a lead to the abandoned warehouse. The door creaking open. Movement too fast to track. Pain. A voice filled with dark amusement: "Welcome to the pack, detective. Time to learn what really happens in your city."

"That attack wasn't sanctioned," Dana said grimly. "There's a rogue element breaking our oldest laws. Forced turning is forbidden under the Accords. But now that you're one of us, you need to understand what you've joined."

She gestured to the victim's wounds. "These marks are deliberate - a message in supernatural language. Similar marks appeared during the Territorial Disputes of 1923, when Sarah Blackwood united vampires, werewolves, and fae against a common threat. Now history's repeating itself, but with modern complications."

The moon climbed higher, its pull becoming irresistible. Ethan's bones began to creak with impending change. Dana checked her watch with practiced calm.

"There's a safe house in the old manufacturing district. I'll tell you about the Blackwood Coalition while you change - how Sarah united traditional enemies against a threat to both supernatural and human worlds. It might help you understand why someone wanted a detective in their pack badly enough to break our most sacred laws."

Pain lanced through Ethan's body, but understanding bloomed alongside it. This wasn't just about becoming a werewolf - he was joining a centuries-old legacy of supernatural peacekeepers, inheriting a history that ran beneath Daybridge's surface like hidden ley lines.

As his bones began their terrible reformation, Dana's voice continued steady and clear, weaving together threads of personal transformation and ancient history. He was becoming part of something larger than himself, a guardian tradition that had shaped Daybridge for generations. The night belonged to both detective and wolf, and somehow, he would learn to be both.

His last human thought, before the change took him completely, was a quiet revelation: He wasn't just solving crimes anymore - he was protecting the delicate balance between worlds, joining a line of guardians stretching back through Daybridge's hidden history. The question was whether he could master both roles before whatever force had turned him unleashed its full plan on the city.

～

CHAPTER TWO

FIRST BLOOD

Rain pelted the Daybridge city streets as Ethan stared at the crime scene photos spread across his desk. The lab results revealed a disturbing cocktail of compounds: artificially engineered lycanthrone-B, modified adrenal stimulants, and "lunar mimetic proteins." His heightened senses picked up Masters' cologne from three desks away, and beneath it all, a familiar metallic scent that made his wolf stir restlessly.

Four bodies in two weeks. All "animal attacks" during the new moon, when werewolves were weakest. The latest lab results showed the same profile - synthetic growth hormone XJ-247, methylated silver compounds, and the mysterious Compound L-13.

Dana Walker materialized beside him. "Blackwood documented these same compounds in 1923. They were trying to create synthetic werewolves - beings who could transform without the moon's influence. The Westbrook Laboratory incident in '89 followed the same pattern. Twenty-seven test subjects died when their bodies rejected the synthetic compounds."

Before Ethan could respond, a new scent hit him - powerful, dominant, mixed with expensive cologne and old money. Stephano Kane strode into the precinct, six-foot-three with silver-streaked dark hair, and eyes that held decades of predatory intelligence. The Alpha of the city's most powerful werewolf pack moved with the casual grace of someone who never questioned their authority.

"Detective Reeves," Kane's voice carried smoothly across the bullpen." Might I have a moment of your time? Regarding the recent... incidents."

Masters raised an eyebrow." You know Kane?"

"We've never met," Ethan said carefully, even as his wolf recognized its superior." But his family's name comes up in a lot of cases." Too many cases, he thought, remembering the files where Kane Industries appeared peripherally, always just beyond the reach of proper investigation.

Kane's smile didn't reach his eyes." Shall we use Interview Room Three? More... private."

The Alpha's presence made Ethan's wolf want to bare its throat.

"What they found in Westbrook's ruins was worse," Kane said, his voice carrying across the bullpen. "Partial successes. "Humans trapped between forms. Just like Blackwood's case - she got too close to the truth before disappearing. They found her badge in the river, along with notes about 'Project CHIMERA.'

In Interview Room Three, Kane's dominance filled the space. "You've been busy, pup. Investigating your own kind while refusing my summons."

"I'm not one of yours," Ethan growled, fighting the instinct to submit. "I'm a cop first." But even as he said it, something deep inside him yearned for pack, for belonging, for the guidance of an experienced Alpha who could teach him to control his new nature.

Kane moved with incredible speed, slamming Ethan against the wall." You're what I say you are. These territories have rules. Hierarchies. The lone wolf act stops now."

"Five dead," Kane corrected, stepping back and straightening his Italian suit." They found another one an hour ago. The Rogue is challenging my authority, using these kills to destabilize my territory. And you, my unwitting new beta, are caught in the middle."

"I'm not your beta."

"No?" Kane's smile was all fangs now." Then why can you feel the pull to obey me? Why does your wolf whimper for pack?" He leaned closer, voice dropping to a whisper." And how long do you think you can solve these murders without access to the supernatural underground? Face it, Detective. You need me."

The door opened, and Masters' voice cut through the tension." Reeves, we've got another body. Downtown."

Kane stepped back, his presence suddenly all business-like charm." Think about what I said, Detective. The full moon's in twenty-seven days. How many more will die before you accept what you are?"

Ethan pushed past him, following Masters out. His hands were shaking again, but not from the lingering effects of transformation. Kane was right - he needed information only the pack could provide. But joining them meant acknowledging he was no longer just a detective. No longer fully human.

The latest victim lay behind the Golden Crown Casino. The body was still fresh, steam rising from the wounds into the cold night air. Three parallel slash marks across the throat - signature of a werewolf kill. But something was different this time.

The forensics showed the same synthetic profile, plus something new - compounds hybridizing werewolf and vampire DNA. The victim bore Kane's pack symbol, still fresh on their wrist.

Ethan crouched beside the body, his nostrils flaring at the scent of artificial hormones. He caught a scent that made his wolf bristle with recognition. This victim was one of them - a werewolf. The Rogue wasn't just killing humans anymore. Someone was perfecting a formula that had claimed lives for generations, drawing closer to creating synthetic supernatural beings that could transcend the natural order.

The rain washed away evidence but not responsibility. His phone buzzed - a text from an unknown number: "The pack runs at midnight. Your territory, your responsibility. Time to choose sides, Detective."

Ethan stared at the message, his thumb hovering over the delete button. The wolf in him howled for pack, for belonging, for the chance to run with others of his kind. The cop in him remembered every suspicious case involving Kane's people, every witness who suddenly became uncooperative, every trail that went cold when it led toward werewolf territory.

He deleted the message, but Kane's words echoed in his mind as they drove toward the latest crime scene. The rain had turned to a heavy downpour, and even through the car windows, his enhanced senses picked up the scent of blood and death.

"Same MO as the others," Masters said, holding an umbrella." But this one's different. Victim's got a tattoo - looks fresh." He pointed to a mark on the victim's wrist: a stylized wolf's head inside a crown. Kane's pack symbol.

Ethan's phone buzzed again: "Still think you can handle this alone, Detective? The pack protects its own. Time's running out."

He stood slowly, rain washing down his face, mixing with the sweat of effort it took to keep his wolf in check around so much blood. The victim had been young, probably newly turned like him. Someone's beta, someone's responsibility. Someone who died alone in an alley because the human world couldn't protect him, and the wolf world wouldn't.

"You okay, Reeves?" Masters' voice was concerned." You look like you've seen a ghost."

"Just thinking," Ethan replied, his voice rough. The scent of Kane's pack was all over the area, but underneath it was something else -

something wild and wrong, a werewolf gone feral, drunk on power and blood. The Rogue's signature.

He had twenty-seven days until the next full moon to decide: solve these murders as a cop or embrace what he'd become and tackle them as a wolf. But as he stared at the dead beta wearing Kane's mark, he wondered if there was a third option - a way to be both protector and predator, bound by duty rather than pack law.

The rain continued to fall, washing away evidence but not responsibility. Somewhere in his city, a killer was moving among humans and wolves alike. And Ethan Reeves, caught between two worlds, had to decide where his loyalties lay before more blood stained the streets.

His wolf howled inside him, demanding pack, demanding belonging. But as he stared at the dead beta wearing Kane's mark, he wondered if there was a third option - a way to be both cop and wolf, protector of both worlds, bound by duty rather than pack law.

The night was young, and somewhere out there, the Rogue was watching, waiting, killing. And Ethan had a terrible feeling that his decision wouldn't wait for twenty-seven days. It would come much sooner, written in blood and moonlight, with lives hanging in the balance.

CHAPTER THREE

PAST SHADOWS

THREE YEARS AGO, when Ethan first encountered Viktor Blackwood, he had no idea he was witnessing just one piece of Daybridge's delicate supernatural power balance. The Blackwood Accord, established in 1923, was a peace treaty between the city's three major supernatural factions: the Blackwood vampire coven, the Kane werewolf pack, and the Thorne witch covenant. The agreement divided Daybridge into territories and established rules for coexistence with humans.

Stephano Kane inherited both his Alpha status and Kane Industries from his mother, Victoria Kane, fifteen years ago. Under her leadership, the pack had transformed from a loose coalition of werewolves into a corporate empire. Kane Industries' real estate holdings and financial investments served a dual purpose - providing cover for pack activities while maintaining control over key territories. What few knew was that Victoria Kane had also inherited something else - detailed records of the Westbrook Laboratory experiments and their connection to Project CHIMERA.

Unlike the old Alpha bloodlines that ruled through brute force, Stephano Kane wielded power through a combination of wealth, political influence, and strategic alliances. His pack members held positions throughout Daybridge's power structure - lawyers, doctors, city officials. This network let him protect pack interests while maintaining the supernatural world's secrecy.

Now, the Blackwood Accord was fracturing. Territorial disputes between vampires and werewolves had escalated into open violence. The Rogue's killings weren't random - they targeted individuals connected to all three factions, threatening to expose the supernatural world to human authorities.

Kane wanted Ethan for three reasons: First, as a police detective, he could help maintain the veil of secrecy. Second, his unusual strength as a newly turned werewolf suggested he had Alpha potential. Third, and most importantly, having a detective in his pack would give Kane an advantage in navigating both human and supernatural laws.

The conflict Ethan found himself in went beyond choosing between his police duties and werewolf nature. The synthetic compounds found in recent victims - lycanthrone-B and Compound L-13 - matched formulas from Victoria Kane's private archives. The same compounds that had been present in Sarah Blackwood's final cases.

Kane was positioning himself to reshape the Blackwood Accord, using the crisis to consolidate power. He needed Ethan not just as a beta, but as a symbol - proof that werewolves could maintain their humanity while embracing their power.

In his office at Kane Tower, Stephano Kane studied old photographs on his wall - his mother standing with Viktor Blackwood and Eleanor Thorne at the Accord's 50th anniversary. Beside them lay Dr. Westbrook's partially recovered research notes, detailing attempts to create synthetic werewolves. The world had changed since then. Supernatural beings couldn't rule through fear alone anymore; they needed to adapt.

"Your mother would have handled this differently," his sister Diana said from the doorway. "She understood why the Westbrook experiments had to be stopped." As Kane Industries' legal counsel and his pack's enforcer, she understood both sides of their world.

"Mother's methods belonged to a different era," Kane replied, touching the silver wolf's head ring that marked him as Alpha." "She couldn't see that controlling the formula means controlling the future. The old ways of territory and tribute aren't enough anymore. We need someone who understands both worlds - someone like Reeves."

"And if he discovers the truth about the lab results? About your involvement?"

Kane's eyes flashed amber." "He won't. The same way no one discovered the truth about Blackwood's disappearance or the Westbrook fire." "The Rogue is forcing everyone to choose sides. When the Accord falls - and it will fall - only those with strong packs will survive what comes next."

The sun set over Daybridge, casting Kane Tower's shadow across the city. Somewhere out there, Ethan Reeves was investigating another death, unaware that the synthetic compounds in the victims' blood came from Kane's own laboratories. The Blackwood Accord was dying, and its death would usher in a new era - one where supernatural power came not from ancient bloodlines, but from carefully engineered formulas.

"Send the message," he told Diana." Let our detective know exactly what's at stake."

In his hands, the silver wolf's head ring caught the last rays of sunlight. His mother had worn it for forty years, maintaining the old balance. But times changed, and so must the packs. Ethan Reeves would learn this truth, one way or another. The only question was whether he would survive the lesson.

CHAPTER FOUR

PACK POLITICS

THE KANE PACK gathered in an unexpected place - the restored Victorian ballroom of the Daybridge Natural History Museum. Ethan's enhanced senses picked up the mingled scents of at least thirty were-wolves as he entered through the private entrance. Old money mixed with new power, corporate wolves in tailored suits alongside those who embraced a more traditional, wild existence.

Claudia Starr met him at the door, her usual white suit replaced by ceremonial pack clothing - dark leather and silver emblems of rank." You came."

"Not joining," Ethan clarified." Just listening."

The gathering formed a loose circle, unconsciously arranging them-selves by pack hierarchy. Kane stood at the center, his sister Diana at his right hand, Claudia moving to take her place at his left. The Alpha's eyes found Ethan lingering at the periphery.

Elder wolf Claudia Starr, who'd survived the Westbrook incident, spoke first. "In 1989, we faced a similar threat. A rogue pack called the Iron Claws tried to seize control by exposing supernatural beings to humans. They worked with corrupted scientists, using early versions of the same compounds we're seeing now."

"The Iron Claws weren't working alone," added Thomas Reid, a gray-haired wolf who'd served as Victoria Kane's adviser. "They had allies in the Thorne covenant - breakaway witches who believed in using synthetic formulas to enhance their powers. Just like Blackwood discovered before she disappeared."

Kane stood at the center, Diana and Claudia flanking him. "Detective Reeves honors us with his presence. Perhaps now he'll understand what's truly at stake."

The reports painted a disturbing picture: financial irregularities, hunter activity, blood bank thefts. Each incident connected to the synthetic compounds found in recent victims - lycanthrone-B and Compound L-13.

One by one, pack members stepped forward to report. A banker describing financial irregularities in vampire-owned businesses. A city council member warned of increased hunter activity. A hospital admin-istrator detailing mysterious blood bank thefts. Each report built a picture of mounting tensions, of ancient balances tipping toward chaos.

Ethan's wolf stirred restlessly as the pieces connected. The synthetic pack markers, the strategic killings, the escalating territorial violations - someone was systematically dismantling the power structures that kept supernatural peace in Daybridge.

"The Thorne covenant reports similar infiltrations," Kane continued." Their wards have been compromised, their prophecies clouded. Even the Blackstone coven has found spies within their ranks."

Claudia Starr spoke again, her voice heavy with memory. "In '93, werewolves and witches united against vampire separatists who'd stolen Westbrook's research. They were creating hybrid soldiers - just like these new victims with mixed supernatural markers. The alliance held then, but the price was high."

Claudia took the floor. "We've identified more executives with synthetic markers. They're using Kane Industries' resources to monitor all factions. But the compounds themselves..." She glanced at Ethan. "They're based on police forensics technology."

"The Rogue isn't working alone," Diana added. "These kills are exposing infiltrators, forcing us into the open."

A young wolf - barely more than a teenager - spoke up." Why not just eliminate them all? Show them our true strength?"

Kane's eyes flashed dangerously." Because, pup, that's exactly what our enemy wants. Open warfare would expose us all, bring down the human authorities in force. In this century, secrets protect us more than strength."

Ethan felt the weight of Kane's words. As a detective, he'd seen how fragile the barrier between worlds really was. One viral video, one undeniable incident, and centuries of careful hiding would unravel.

Claudia took the floor, her presence commanding attention." We've identified more executives with synthetic markers. They're using Kane Industries' resources to monitor all three factions. But the compounds themselves..." She glanced at Ethan." They're based on police forensics technology. Someone with access to law enforcement resources is helping coordinate this."

The implications hit Ethan like a physical blow. Someone in the department, someone with access to his cases, was working against both human and supernatural law. His two worlds weren't just colliding - they were being deliberately smashed together.

"The Rogue isn't working alone," Diana Kane added." These kills are too precise, too strategic. They're exposing the infiltrators to force us into the open, make us reveal ourselves in retaliation."

The young wolf spoke again: "So we find this Rogue and—"

"And what?" Ethan spoke. "Kill them? Add another body to the pile? Create more evidence for my colleagues to find?"

The room fell silent. Kane's eyes gleamed with approval - he'd been waiting for Ethan to engage.

"Detective Reeves makes a valid point," Kane said. "We must be smarter than our enemies. Which is why we need people who understand both worlds. People who can walk the line between human law and pack justice."

Ethan felt the weight of every gaze in the room. His wolf responded to the pull of pack, the promise of belonging, while his human side remembered his oath to serve and protect all citizens - human and supernatural.

Claudia approached him, speaking softly." You're not betraying your badge by acknowledging what you are. The choice isn't between human and wolf - it's between order and chaos."

After the gathering, Ethan sat in his car outside the museum, studying crime scene photos on his phone. The victims weren't random. Each death exposed another thread in the conspiracy, another pressure point in Daybridge's supernatural power structure. The Rogue was forcing everyone to choose sides, but the real question was: what happened when there were no more sides to choose?

His phone buzzed - a text from Masters: "We need to talk about the Kane Industries cases. Something bigger going on. Watch your back."

In the rearview mirror, his eyes flickered between human brown and wolf amber. The badge on his belt felt heavier than ever. Kane was right about one thing - someone was using him, using his position as both cop and werewolf to engineer a collision between worlds.

The question wasn't whether he would choose a side. The question was whether he could create a third option before Daybridge erupted into supernatural war with humans caught in the crossfire.

Claudia's words echoed in his mind: The choice isn't between human and wolf - it's between order and chaos.

But as he started his car, another thought surfaced: What if maintaining order required embracing a little chaos first?

The streets of Daybridge stretched before him, human and supernatural worlds existing in careful balance. For now. But with each passing night, that balance grew more precarious, and Ethan Reeves - detective, werewolf, and reluctant bridge between worlds - had decisions to make that would affect both sides of his divided city.

CHAPTER FIVE

THE GATHERING DARK

THE CRIMSON CELLAR looked like any other upscale Daybridge nightclub from the outside - sleek, modern, with a line of hopeful patrons stretching around the block. But Claudia led Ethan through a side entrance marked with subtle symbols he now recognized as supernatural wards.

"Welcome to neutral ground," she said, guiding him into what seemed to be a converted warehouse space beneath the main club." The one place in Daybridge where all factions can meet without violating territorial agreements."

The space defied easy description. Victorian furniture mixed with modern tech. Witches in business suits sat alongside vampires in vintage clothing. Werewolves from different packs mingled cautiously at a long bar where the bartender - who smelled neither human nor any other species Ethan could identify - mixed drinks that occasionally glowed.

"Detective Reeves," a familiar voice called. Viktor Blackwood approached, looking exactly as he had three years ago in that basement." Finally joining the night crowd properly?"

"He's here as an observer," Claudia answered before Ethan could speak." Kane's orders."

"Ah yes, your new Alpha." Viktor's smile didn't reach his eyes." Though I remember when you were quite interested in vampire cases, Detective."

A woman materialized beside Marcus - literally materialized, Ethan realized with a start. Her business suit was impeccably pressed, her gray hair tied in a severe bun." Eleanor Thorne," she introduced herself." Covenant Leader. We've been watching your progression with interest."

"The police detective who became a werewolf," another voice added. A young man with silver-white hair and pupilless eyes lounged near-by." Quite the story in certain circles. I'm Ash. No last name, no faction. Information broker."

Ethan's senses were overwhelmed. Every corner of the room held new supernatural signatures. A group of people with subtle scales beneath their skin. A woman whose shadow moved independently of her body. Beings that seemed to shift form when viewed from different angles.

"Overwhelming, isn't it?" Claudia's voice anchored him." Even born wolves need time to adjust to this place."

"How long has this been here?"

"The Crimson Cellar? Since Daybridge's founding. Every city with a significant supernatural population has one. A neutral zone where information can be traded, deals made, politics discussed without starting wars."

Eleanor Thorne gestured to a private booth. "Perhaps we should discuss recent events somewhere more... discrete."

The booth's privacy wards activated as they sat, creating a bubble of silence. Viktor and Ash joined them, along with a woman Claudia introduced as Marina James - Thomas James's widow and a prominent member of the city's supernatural business community.

"The synthetic pack markers were just the beginning," Marina said, her grief evident but controlled." Someone is systematically targeting all three major factions. My husband discovered evidence of similar synthetic compounds being developed to mimic vampire thrall and witch bloodlines."

"Impossible," Eleanor interrupted." Magical bloodlines can't be synthesized."

"Three years ago, we would have said the same about pack bonds," Viktor pointed out. "Technology is catching up to magic faster than we'd like to admit."

Ash spread several photographs across the table. "These were taken at different supernatural gatherings across the city. Note the markers I've highlighted."

Ethan studied the images. In each one, certain individuals had subtle wrong notes in their posture, their interactions. Like actors who had studied their roles well but couldn't quite nail the performance.

"How many?" he asked.

"At least thirty confirmed infiltrators," Ash replied. "Probably more that can't be identified. They're in corporations, government offices, police departments—"

"The police?" Ethan's wolf stirred uneasily.

"Your partner's been asking questions," Marina said quietly. "The right questions, from the wrong perspective. Someone's pointing him toward the supernatural world but making sure he sees us as threats."

A commotion at the bar drew their attention. Two younger werewolves - one Kane pack, one from a smaller coalition - were squaring off. The bartender's hands began to glow with warning light.

"Tensions are rising," Eleanor observed. "The infiltrators are pushing us toward exposure, and the younger ones are eager for confrontation."

"They don't remember the last supernatural war," Viktor Blackwood added grimly. "They never saw what happened when humans discovered us in numbers."

The Crimson Cellar's atmosphere had shifted, becoming charged with potential violence. Ethan saw it through new eyes - vampires withdrawing to shadows, witches strengthening personal wards, werewolves unconsciously grouping by pack.

"Your position is unique, Detective," Eleanor said. "You bridge both worlds naturally now. The question is: will you help us maintain the balance, or will you be the catalyst for its destruction?"

Before Ethan could answer, his phone buzzed. A text from Masters: "Another body. This one's different. You need to see this."

Claudia read the message over his shoulder. "Go. But remember what you've seen here. Remember that exposure doesn't just mean chaos for us - it means danger for humans too. How many innocent people will die if supernatural warfare spills onto Daybridge's streets?"

As Ethan left The Crimson Cellar, he passed the two young werewolves, now being firmly separated by their respective pack members. Their anger felt personal, but he recognized the larger forces at work - friction created by unseen hands, pushing the supernatural world toward a breaking point.

His phone buzzed again. Crime scene details. The victim was someone he'd seen in The Crimson Cellar - one of the scaled people, now found publicly displayed in Daybridge Central Park.

The game was escalating. The Rogue wasn't just killing now; they were sending messages. And as Ethan headed toward another crime scene, he realized he was no longer just a detective investigating supernatural crimes. He was becoming a player in a game where the stakes were nothing less than the exposure of an entire hidden world.

Behind him, The Crimson Cellar's discrete entrance vanished into shadow, its supernatural patrons continuing their ancient dance of politics and power, while somewhere in Daybridge, architects of chaos pushed the city closer to a war that would destroy both human and supernatural lives.

The crime scene photos revealed Saren N'Vex's body in horrific detail. The victim's partial transformation had been chemically induced - their scaled form trapped between states. The ritualistic cuts formed patterns that merged occult symbolism with molecular diagrams. Under UV light, the wounds fluoresced, suggesting the killer had introduced compounds designed to interact with supernatural biology.

Marina pulled up molecular analyses on her tablet. "The synthetic compounds share a striking foundation. They're all built on modified neurotransmitter chains, similar to what's used in classified military behavioral modification programs. Project CHIMERA specifically - supposedly discontinued in 2018."

Ash spread photographs across the table. The infiltrators' movements revealed their training - the way they maintained sightlines, their tactical positioning in crowds. But their bloodwork told the real story. Each synthetic compound shared a base structure derived from military combat enhancement drugs, modified with supernatural genetic markers.

"The vampire thrall simulation uses a compound that affects the parasympathetic nervous system," Viktor Blackwood explained, studying the data. "It mimics the biochemical bonds created by vampire blood, but it's engineered using components from truth serums and loyalty conditioning protocols."

Marina highlighted financial trails linking Kane Industries to military research subsidiaries. "Thomas discovered unauthorized transfers to a black site laboratory. Project designation: PROMETHEUS. They're using supernatural genetic samples to develop enhanced soldier programs."

The witch bloodline replication proved even more disturbing. The infiltrators carried nanotech that could interfere with magical energy fields - technology that shared patents with experimental police crowd control devices. But the synthetic compounds in their systems suggested something more - attempts to artificially recreate magical affinities.

Ethan's phone lit up with Masters' message about the confidential informant. Cross-referencing the contact details against Kane Industries personnel records revealed a connection - Dr. Barbara Kelly, Thomas James's research partner and the last person to see him alive.

"The infiltrators aren't just gathering intelligence," Eleanor said, examining the patterns cut into Saren's body. "These are test protocols. They're documenting how supernatural traits can be synthesized, measuring biological responses to forced transformation."

Marina's tablet displayed internal Kane Industries security protocols. "The infiltrators have been systematically altering patrol patterns, creating gaps in surveillance. But the changes required high-level access codes - codes only Thomas James and Dr. Barbara Kelly had clearance to use."

The chemical analyses painted a chilling picture. Each synthetic compound represented an attempt to recreate supernatural abilities through scientific means. The werewolf markers contained modified K-9 training compounds combined with experimental combat enhancement drugs. Vampire thrall simulation used neurotransmitter manipulation derived from military loyalty programming. Witch bloodline replication involved nanotech that could disrupt energy fields.

"Your partner's investigation," Claudia noted, "follows the exact paths where evidence of these programs has been deliberately left. Scientific explanations for supernatural phenomena, hints of military involvement, corporate conspiracy. The perfect trail to convince law enforcement they're dealing with illegal human experimentation rather than actual supernatural beings."

Masters' latest message carried more urgency: "Meeting Dr. Kelly tonight. Says she has proof of illegal medical testing at Kane Industries. Military connection confirmed."

The Crimson Cellar's atmosphere grew thick with tension as news of Saren's death spread. The killer hadn't just taken a life - they'd demonstrated their ability to manipulate supernatural biology at its most fundamental level. Each death revealed another aspect of their research, another step toward synthetic replication of supernatural traits.

The infiltrators moved through supernatural society with practiced ease, their artificial markers good enough to fool casual detection. But their true purpose wasn't just surveillance - they were test subjects, proving that humans could be modified to mimic supernatural abilities.

Project PROMETHEUS's goals became clearer: creating synthetic supernatural soldiers, combining military enhancement protocols with replicated supernatural traits. Kane Industries' involvement suggested access to both supernatural genetic material and military research facilities.

Dr. Barbara Kelly's role as informant raised alarming questions. Her research with Thomas had focused on biochemical markers - exactly the kind of work needed to develop synthetic supernatural compounds. Was she exposing the program, or leading Masters toward a carefully crafted revelation?

Ethan's world of evidence and procedure collided with supernatural politics and advanced biochemistry. The killer wasn't just targeting random supernatural beings - they were eliminating witnesses to a program that could fundamentally change the balance of power between humans and supernatural beings.

As they prepared to examine Saren's body, Ethan realized the true stakes. Someone wasn't just trying to expose the supernatural world - they were learning to replicate it, to control it, to perhaps replace it entirely. The question wasn't just who was behind it all, but what kind of world they planned to create with their army of synthetic supernatural soldiers.

The endgame wouldn't just expose supernatural beings - it would make them obsolete. And somewhere in Daybridge, Dr. Barbara Kelly was preparing to tell Masters just enough truth to set that endgame in motion.

CHAPTER SIX

HISTORICAL ECHOES

IN THE PRIVATE archives beneath Kane Tower, Ethan found himself surrounded by centuries of supernatural history. Diana Kane moved purposefully through the climate-controlled vault, pulling leather-bound volumes and preservation-sealed documents.

"Sebastian Vale's original research," she explained, laying out a journal dated 1872. The pages were filled with intricate molecular drawings that somehow merged with occult symbols. "He wasn't just an alchemist - he was a visionary who saw no distinction between science and magic."

The journal detailed Vale's progression: first studying werewolf transformation through chemical analysis, then attempting to isolate vampire thrall compounds, finally trying to synthesize witch bloodline markers. The similarities to the current crisis were chilling.

"Vale believed supernatural power was simply advanced biochemistry," Eleanor Thorne added, her fingers tracing the ancient formulas. "He created the first synthetic werewolf in 1871 - a partial success that lived for three days before its enhanced biology tore it apart."

Viktor Blackwood materialized from the shadows, holding a stack of yellowed newspapers. "The public records called it the 'Daybridge Beast Murders.' Fourteen supernatural beings killed, their bodies drained of blood and essence. Vale needed raw materials for his experiments."

The archived photos showed ceremonial killing grounds similar to their current crime scenes - molecular diagrams merged with occult symbols, victims positioned to channel energy. Even the chemical markers found in modern victims echoed Vale's original compounds.

"But Vale wasn't working alone," Diana continued, revealing military documents from the 1870s. "He had government funding through the Department of Strategic Resources - the predecessor to Project CHIMERA. They wanted supernatural soldiers even then."

Eleanor unrolled an ancient map of Daybridge marked with ley lines and power nodes. "Vale chose his victims and locations carefully, creating a grid of supernatural energy he could tap. The modern killings follow the same pattern - they're recreating his work with advanced technology."

"The Alchemist's Rebellion ended in fire," Viktor said quietly. "Vale's laboratory exploded, taking three city blocks with it. The official story blamed a gas main rupture. The truth was far worse - he successfully created a hybrid being that couldn't contain its own power."

Diana pulled up modern satellite imagery on her tablet, overlaying it with Vale's energy grid. The new killing sites aligned perfectly with his original pattern. "They're not just copying his research - they're completing it. Dr. Winters worked in the same laboratory space Vale used, built over the ruins of his original facility."

"There's more," Eleanor added. "In 1923, another scientist continued Vale's work – Emma Lacey. She discovered his hidden records and realized someone in the government was still pursuing his research. That's why she disappeared."

"And Elena Westbrook in 1989," Viktor continued. "Each generation, someone rediscovers Vale's work and tries to perfect it. Each time, we stop them. But they keep getting closer to success."

Ethan studied the historical documents, seeing how Vale's crude attempts at supernatural synthesis laid the groundwork for Project CHIMERA and PROMETHEUS. The modern killers weren't just copying an old experiment - they were building on centuries of forbidden research.

"Vale believed science could control supernatural power," Eleanor explained. "But he didn't understand that our abilities aren't just biological - they're connected to fundamental forces. Try to replicate them artificially, and those forces become unstable."

Diana's tablet displayed thermal imaging of recent crime scenes, showing energy patterns identical to those in Vale's journals. "They've solved the biological problems that killed Vale's creations. But they still haven't accounted for the metaphysical backlash."

"That's why they need Ethan," Viktor realized. "A police detective who successfully transformed - proof that someone can bridge the scientific and supernatural worlds without losing control."

The archives held one final revelation - Vale's last journal entry, written the night his laboratory exploded: "They think I am creating weapons, but I am creating evolution itself. The fusion of science and supernatural will birth a new species - one that transcends all natural laws."

As Ethan left the archives, the historical weight pressed down on him. Vale's hubris had nearly exposed the supernatural world. Now, over a century later, his intellectual descendants were on the verge of succeeding where he failed - unless they could be stopped by someone who understood both worlds.

The night air carried the scent of rain and destiny. Somewhere in Daybridge, Dr. Winters was preparing to meet Masters, carrying secrets that could shatter the barrier between worlds. History was poised to repeat itself, unless Ethan could find a way to break a cycle that began with an alchemist's dark dreams of synthetic divinity.

CHAPTER SEVEN

THE OLD CASES

THE PRECINCT'S FLUORESCENT lights flickered as Ethan reviewed the Blackwood files. Viktor Blackwood's coven wasn't just wealthy - they were power brokers, maintaining delicate alliances between vampire houses while mediating supernatural diplomatic relations. Their corporate empire provided cover for supernatural activities: blood banks disguised as medical research facilities, properties strategically placed along ley lines, security firms staffed by vampire enforcers.

The Morgan case files revealed deeper connections. What he'd thought was corporate espionage had actually been a power struggle between Blackwood's coven and the Rising Dawn vampire house. Morgan had violated ancient treaties by selling vampire blood on the human black market. His partner - the witch Ethan had arrested - had been acting as supernatural executioner, delivering justice according to codes older than human law.

Studying his case history chronologically, patterns emerged:

Supernatural incidents clustered around celestial events - not just full moons, but astronomical alignments that affected magical energy. The Chinatown disappearances had coincided with a rare planetary conjunction. The Antiquities Thefts followed ancient ritual calendars.

Territorial disputes followed predictable cycles. Vampire houses relocated hunting grounds every seven years. Werewolf packs adjusted territories during specific lunar phases. Witch covens performed boundary rites on seasonal equinoxes. What looked like random crime sprees were actually choreographed supernatural power shifts.

The victims fit patterns too. The Waterfront Murders targeted vampires who'd violated feeding restrictions. The Warehouse District Maulings involved werewolves who'd threatened pack secrecy. Each "random" crime maintained supernatural order.

His phone chimed with messages:

Masters: "Connecting dots between cold cases. These rich families - Blackwood, Kane, Thorne - they're connected to every major unsolved case."

Claudia: "Kane needs your insight on jurisdiction conflicts. Supernatural justice system failing to contain threats."

The Blackwood coven's true role became clearer through archived reports. They weren't just powerful - they were peacekeepers. Their corporate network provided infrastructure for supernatural governance: secure meeting places, diplomatic channels, information networks. When that system worked, supernatural crimes remained invisible to human authorities.

But now that system was breaking down. The synthetic infiltrators weren't just disrupting power structures - they were overwhelming the supernatural justice system's ability to self-police. Each exposed crime threatened centuries of careful secrecy.

Ethan pulled up his latest case notes, outlining a new approach:

For human justice: Document everything but encode supernatural elements in plausible deniability. Build cases that could stand up in human courts without exposing the hidden world. Use his police authority to protect crime scenes long enough for supernatural cleanup crews to remove compromising evidence.

For supernatural justice: Leverage his police access to monitor both worlds. Watch for patterns indicating larger threats. Build trust with supernatural factions while maintaining his human law enforcement role. Create protocols for handling cases that crossed between worlds.

The Blackwood coven's archives, which he now had limited access to, revealed historical precedents. Other law enforcement officers had straddled both worlds before, serving as unofficial liaisons. Some had succeeded in maintaining balance. Others had been destroyed by the attempt.

His phone buzzed again. Viktor Blackwood: "The coven has voted. We're prepared to formally recognize your dual authority, with conditions. Meet tonight."

The implications were significant. Official recognition from one of Daybridge's most powerful supernatural factions would give him legitimate authority in both worlds. But it would also bind him to ancient laws and obligations he was only beginning to understand.

The old cases had prepared him for this moment, each "impossible" solution teaching him to navigate between worlds. Now he needed to formalize that role, create sustainable systems for managing supernatural crime without exposing supernatural society.

Studying the patterns revealed three critical factors:

Timing: Supernatural crimes followed ancient rhythms. Understanding these cycles could help prevent conflicts before they erupt.

Territory: Most supernatural violence stemmed from boundary disputes. Creating clear jurisdictional guidelines between human and supernatural authorities could reduce conflicts.

Politics: Every supernatural crime had political implications. Managing those politics required understanding centuries-old alliances and enmities.

A new case file landed on his desk - apparent suicide, prominent business figure, locked room. Once he would have seen only the human elements. Now he recognized signs of supernatural involvement:

residual magical energy, traces of vampire thrall, werewolf territorial markers.

This was the test case for his new approach. Could he solve it in a way that satisfied both justice systems? Could he maintain human law while respecting supernatural sovereignty?

The old cases had taught him to see beyond surface explanations. Now he needed to apply those lessons to build bridges between worlds - before the rising tide of synthetic infiltrators and exposed supernatural activity destroyed both systems of justice.

His phone lit up one final time. Diana Kane: "The pack is monitoring your progress. Don't make us regret supporting this experiment."

No pressure, then. Just the future of supernatural-human relations in Daybridge resting on his ability to successfully navigate both worlds. The old cases had brought him to this point. The new ones would determine whether coexistence was possible, or if both systems of justice would collapse under the weight of exposure.

Time to prove that impossible cases could have possible solutions - even if those solutions required walking the razor's edge between human law and supernatural justice.

CHAPTER EIGHT
TERRITORY

The warehouse air grew thick with tension as Ethan made rapid decisions. He photographed the supernatural markers, logging them in an encrypted drive only supernatural authorities could access. The claw marks and impact craters would remain - explainable as signs of violent struggle to human investigators. But the runic boundaries and pack markings disappeared under carefully applied luminol, visible now only to enhanced senses.

Thomas James' research had to be preserved but protected. Ethan split the evidence: The shipping manifests showing chemical compounds went to human evidence logs. The notes on synthetic pack markers, written in ancient werewolf cipher, vanished into Diana's possession. Each piece of evidence carefully categorized to tell necessary truths to both worlds.

"Detective Reeves." Masters' flashlight beam cut through the darkness. "Wait - is that Diana Kane? What's the head of Kane Industries doing at a murder scene?"

"Corporate security concern," Ethan answered smoothly, years of detective work making the half-truth sound natural. "The victim worked for their R&D division."

Behind Masters, Ethan caught the scent of unfamiliar wolves - Red River pack members watching from the shadows, testing how he'd handle the intersection of his duties.

The chemical evidence demanded immediate action. The synthetic compounds were being moved through a network of seemingly legitimate pharmaceutical companies. Ethan could track the human supply chain through official channels while supernatural allies monitored pack movements.

"The shipping manifests show a pattern," he told Masters, careful to focus on the human elements. "Someone's using Kane Industries' distribution network to move experimental compounds."

What he didn't mention were the traces of synthetic pack markers in the victim's blood work, or how the chemical signatures matched samples found in previous infiltrator cases. That evidence went to Marina for supernatural analysis.

The confrontation with Red River pack came three nights later. They caught him leaving a crime scene - six wolves emerging from the shadows, led by their Alpha, Corbin Reed. Their eyes gleamed with synthetic enhancement, their movements showing military precision.

"Detective," Reed's voice carried artificial pack authority. "Time to discuss jurisdiction."

"Jurisdiction's clear," Ethan replied, noting how their synthetic markers affected their pack dynamics. Their movements were too coordinated, lacking the natural chaos of true wolf behavior. "This is Kane territory."

"Territory changes." Reed circled, his pack following in unnaturally perfect formation. "The old ways are dying, Detective. Synthetic enhancement is the future. We're offering you a chance to be part of it."

The fight erupted without warning. Reed's pack moved with programmed efficiency, but their synthetic nature made them predictable. Ethan's genuine wolf instincts recognized patterns in their enhanced movements.

He didn't fight alone. Claudia emerged from concealment, her natural wolf speed outmaneuvering their artificial enhancement. Diana's presence blazed with true Alpha power, overwhelming their synthetic pack dynamics.

The battle revealed crucial intelligence: The synthetic compounds gave them enhanced strength but limited adaptability. They fought like programmed units, not true wolves. Each movement followed combat algorithms rather than instinct.

Reed fell back, his synthetic pack retreating in precise formation. "This isn't over, Detective. The old boundaries won't hold. Change is coming to Daybridge."

"They're right about change," Diana said afterward, studying samples from the conflict. "But not the way they think. The synthetic compounds are flawed - they enhance abilities but destroy pack bonds. Real wolf packs adapt. These artificial ones can only follow programming."

The warehouse case crystallized Ethan's approach to cross-jurisdiction evidence: Document everything, but filter what each side could safely know. Human authorities followed money trails and shipping manifests. Supernatural allies tracked pack movements and synthetic markers.

Masters' investigation revealed corporate smuggling and illegal medical research. The supernatural investigation uncovered synthetic infiltration and threatened pack territories. Both threads led toward the same conspiracy, approached from different angles.

"Your partner's good," Claudia noted, watching Masters connect pieces of human evidence. "He's going to find the synthetic production facilities. The question is: What will he make of what he finds?"

The Red River confrontation had exposed weaknesses in synthetic enhancement but also revealed their strategic goal: Force supernatural politics into human awareness, using artificial pack members to overwhelm traditional territories.

Ethan's phone filled with updates:

Marina: Chemical analysis showed degrading synthetic markers. The compounds were unstable.

Viktor Blackwood: Vampire houses reporting similar synthetic infiltration attempts.

Eleanor: Witch covens detecting artificial energy signatures.

The warehouse murder had sparked a deeper investigation. Red River pack wasn't just challenging territory - they were testing synthetic combat units, using pack conflicts to gather performance data.

Ethan documented everything in parallel: Official police reports focused on corporate crime and medical research violations. Supernatural records tracked synthetic infiltration and pack boundary challenges. Each investigation supported the other without exposing what needed to remain hidden.

The confrontation with Red River pack had set precedent: Supernatural justice could work alongside human law enforcement, each system handling what it was best equipped to address. The challenge wasn't choosing between worlds but knowing how to let them complement each other.

Diana's words echoed as Ethan filed his reports: "Territory isn't just land anymore. It's about maintaining boundaries between worlds while building bridges where needed."

The warehouse remained a crime scene under human law, a territorial marker in supernatural politics, and a warning of threats facing both worlds. Ethan's role wasn't to choose sides, but to ensure both systems of justice could function without destroying each other.

Red River pack had forced the issue, but they'd also revealed the path forward. True justice meant preserving necessary boundaries while building new frameworks for cooperation between worlds. The synthetic threat had changed the game - now supernatural and human authorities would have to adapt together or fall separately.

CHAPTER NINE

DEPARTMENT SCRUTINY

The downtown killing hit Ethan's desk with Reynolds watching his every move. The victim, found in the financial district, displayed classic vampire feeding marks - but the bloodwork showed traces of synthetic compounds. A hybrid case that would test his ability to investigate under scrutiny.

"What's your first move, Detective?" Reynolds asked, noting his reactions as he studied crime scene photos.

Ethan developed a dual-track approach:

For Human Investigation: Document the Corporate Connections. The Victim, Saren N'Vex, worked for a Pharmaceutical Company Linked to Synthetic Compound Production. Follow Money Trails, Establish Corporate Motives, Build a Case That Would Satisfy Department Oversight.

For Supernatural Investigation: Use Enhanced Senses to Track Vampire Feeding Patterns While Appearing to Examine Conventional Evidence. Code Supernatural Findings in Legitimate Forensic Language. "Unusual Blood Coagulation" Instead of Vampire Feeding. "Chemical Residue" Rather Than Magical Traces.

"Starting with the blood work," he told Reynolds, careful to focus on elements that would register as normal police procedure. "The victim showed unusual chemical markers consistent with experimental drug trials."

His phone buzzed quietly:

Marina: "Victim was investigating synthetic blood production."

Claudia: "Red River pack members spotted near crime scene."

Viktor Blackwood: "Rogue vampire using synthetic compounds. Threatens feeding treaties."

Each message highlighted the impossible balance he had to maintain. The case wasn't just about solving a murder - it was about preventing supernatural exposure while satisfying increasing department scrutiny.

Reynolds shadowed his investigation, documenting every move. "Interesting how you knew to check those specific security cameras. Almost like you knew the killer's escape route."

Because he could smell vampire traces. Because supernatural witnesses had provided information he couldn't officially cite. Because solving the case meant following evidence he couldn't explain to human authorities.

The Impossible Choice

Ethan stood at the crossroads of two justice systems, each path forward carrying devastating consequences. Following human law meant exposing centuries of supernatural secrecy. The department's thorough investigation would uncover vampire feeding grounds, triggering a cascade of revelations. Government agencies would descend upon the synthetic compound research, unraveling the careful fabric of super-natural society. Both justice systems would collapse into chaos as ancient secrets spilled into public view.

Yet choosing supernatural law carried its own heavy price. Abandoning his police responsibilities would leave human authorities vulnerable to synthetic infiltration. Without his unique position bridging both worlds, innocent citizens would lose a crucial protector. His carefully cultivated role allowing oversight of both realms would vanish, potentially leading to unguided police investigations stumbling into supernatural territory.

The solution crystallized through careful navigation of both paths. He began documenting the synthetic compound production through legitimate police channels, constructing a human case focused on corporate espionage and illegal drug trials. This allowed department resources to track the business conspiracy while maintaining necessary secrets.

Working parallel tracks, he coordinated with supernatural allies to contain the rogue vampire and investigate synthetic blood production. His police authority provided crucial scene control, buying time for supernatural cleanup teams to remove compromising evidence before human investigators arrived.

This delicate balance became his template for future cases - building truthful investigations that served justice while preserving essential secrets. Each piece of evidence carefully channeled investigators toward conclusions that protected both worlds while still serving justice. The synthetic compound case proved that the gap between human and supernatural law could be bridged through careful orchestration and precise control of information flow.

Through this dual approach, Ethan discovered that choosing between human and supernatural law was never truly necessary. The real skill lay in finding paths that honored both while compromising neither. His position between worlds wasn't a liability - it was the key to maintaining balance in an increasingly complex reality.

Double Lives

"Your timeline has gaps," Reynolds noted, reviewing his case notes in the precinct's fluorescent-lit interview room. "Two hours unaccounted for last night between 11 PM and 1 AM."

Ethan kept his expression neutral, remembering the actual events: tracking a rogue vampire through The Crimson Cellar's back channels, coordinating with Viktor Blackwood's security teams as they prevented a mass feeding incident at Daybridge General Hospital's blood bank. The vampire had been young, desperate, driven mad by synthetic compounds in their system.

"Canvassing witnesses near Kane Tower," he replied, the practiced lie coming easily now. "Checking security footage from surrounding businesses. Standard procedure."

Reynolds nodded, but his eyes held suspicion. "And the marks on your arm? Looks like claw wounds."

"Caught it on a fence checking a possible entry point." Another smooth deception, covering the reality of restraining a vampire driven feral by experimental drugs.

His official report would show methodical detective work: Witness statements from carefully coached supernatural contacts passing as ordinary citizens. Security footage edited by Kane Industries' tech team to remove evidence of supernatural speed and strength. Physical evidence collected and filtered through layers of procedural obscurity.

"You're spending a lot of time around Kane Industries cases," Reynolds pressed. "Any particular reason?"

Because Stephano Kane's corporate empire was a front for werewolf pack activities. Because vampires were using hospital supply chains to hide blood trafficking. Because witches were concealing magical disturbances behind bureaucratic paperwork.

"Following the evidence," Ethan said simply. "Lot of connections keep leading back there."

His desk calendar showed normal detective routines - witness interviews, evidence processing, report writing. It didn't show pack meetings in hidden venues, supernatural crime scene investigations conducted under cover of darkness, coordinated efforts to maintain the veil between worlds.

"Masters is asking questions," Reynolds warned. "About your changing case closure methods. About why suspects seem to disappear rather than face charges."

Because some suspects needed supernatural justice rather than human courts. Because maintaining secrecy sometimes meant letting the pack or coven handle their own. Because some crimes couldn't be prosecuted without exposing an entire hidden world.

"I adapt my methods to each case," Ethan replied carefully. "Sometimes alternative resolution is more effective than traditional prosecution."

His phone buzzed - a message from Claudia about another synthetic victim found near the docks. But his official response would wait until Reynolds finished the interview, maintaining the careful illusion of normal police work.

"The department's watching you, Reeves," Reynolds said finally. "Make sure your paperwork stays clean."

Ethan nodded, already mentally composing the sanitized version of events that would appear in official records. The supernatural world operated in the shadows of human bureaucracy, and maintaining that shadow meant becoming an expert in selective truth.

As he left the interview room, his phone buzzed again - Diana Kane warning about increased hunter activity near The Crimson Cellar. Tonight, would require more careful balancing, more strategic omissions, more navigation between his sworn duties and supernatural obligations.

The precinct hummed with normal activity - officers filing reports, detectives reviewing cases, the machinery of human law enforcement grinding forward. None of them knew about the parallel investigations happening in darkness, the supernatural crimes hidden behind ordinary incident reports, the careful dance of maintaining two forms of justice.

Ethan's desk calendar showed a simple notation for tonight: "Follow up on witness statements." It didn't mention the pack meeting at midnight, the vampire council's request for assistance, or the growing synthetic threat that straddled both his worlds.

His official case files were masterpieces of strategic omission, telling truths that hid deeper truths. Each report balanced human law with supernatural necessity, maintaining the illusion of normal police work while serving both forms of justice.

As night fell over Daybridge, Ethan prepared for another shift of double duty - human detective by bureaucratic record, supernatural peacekeeper in reality. His badge reflected fluorescent light, while his wolf stirred beneath the surface, both sides of his nature adapted to lives lived in parallel.

The truth was in the gaps - the unwritten hours, the carefully worded reports, the strategic silences that maintained the barrier between worlds. And as Ethan headed out into another night of dual purpose, he knew those gaps were necessary sacrifices in service of a greater peace.

CHAPTER TEN

THE ART OF HIDDEN TRUTH – ETHAN'S TEMPLATE

ETHAN SAT in his apartment's home office, surrounded by two sets of case files. On the left, the official police reports - meticulously crafted documents that would withstand any departmental review. On the right, his private supernatural records, detailing the true nature of Daybridge's hidden crimes.

He opened his laptop to a document titled "Investigation Protocol Alpha" - his evolving template for documenting supernatural cases within human parameters:

EVIDENCE CLASSIFICATION SYSTEM

Level 1: Direct Observable Evidence

- Crime scene photos (excluding supernatural elements)

- Physical evidence with plausible scientific explanation

- Witness statements from vetted human sources

Level 2: Coded Supernatural Elements

- Ritual markings → "Distinct chemical patterns"

- Magical residue → "Trace energy signatures"

- Pack territory markers → "Biological compounds of unknown origin"

Level 3: Protected Information

- Supernatural witness statements

- Magical forensics

- Pack/Coven/Council involvement

The Saren N'Vex case exemplified his system's effectiveness. The official file documented a homicide with unusual chemical compounds present. Chemical analysis reports - carefully edited by Kane Industries' labs - showed "experimental biochemical agents" rather than synthetic supernatural markers. Witness statements came from carefully coached supernatural contacts who could pass as ordinary citizens.

His private records told the full story:

CASE CROSS-REFERENCE SYSTEM

Official Cause of Death: "Chemical exposure leading to cellular breakdown"

Actual Cause: Forced transformation via synthetic compounds

Official Evidence Log:

- Chemical residue on victim → Synthetic pack markers

- UV-reactive trace elements → Magical binding agents

- Tissue degradation → Failed supernatural transformation

Witness Statements:

Public Record: "Anonymous source familiar with victim's work"

Actual Source: Elder vampire from Blackwood's council

Investigation Timeline:

Official: Standard canvassing and lab work

Actual: Supernatural tracking + magical forensics

He'd developed specialized language for each supernatural faction:

TERMINOLOGY PROTOCOLS

Werewolf Cases:

- Pack activities → "Group behavioral patterns"

- Territory markers → "Biological compounds"

- Alpha authority → "Organizational hierarchy"

Vampire Cases:

- Blood feeding → "Biological resource acquisition"

- Thrall influence → "Psychological conditioning"

- Covenant laws → "Traditional behavioral codes"

Witch Cases:

- Spell residue → "Energy discharge patterns"

- Magical wards → "Environmental security measures"

- Coven politics → "Cultural organization structures"

The system extended to crime scene documentation:

SCENE PROCESSING GUIDELINES

1. Initial Documentation

- Standard photos for official file

- Supernatural-sensitive photos for private records

- UV spectrum imaging for magical traces

2. Evidence Collection

- Dual sampling: human lab + supernatural analysis

- Chain of custody documentation with coded notations

- Separate storage protocols for magical items

3. Witness Management

- Pre-interview preparation for supernatural contacts

- Coded statement templates

- Verification through both human + supernatural channels

His latest innovation was a database linking supernatural incidents to plausible human explanations:

INCIDENT CLASSIFICATION MATRIX

Type A: Violence/Physical Damage

- Supernatural combat → "Gang activity"

- Magical explosions → "Gas main rupture"

- Territory disputes → "Corporate rivalry"

Type B: Unusual Deaths

- Failed transformations → "Unknown toxin exposure"

- Magical backlash → "Unexplained energy discharge"

- Feeding incidents → "Rare blood disorder"

Type C: Supernatural Phenomena

- Visible magic → "Atmospheric anomalies"

- Public transformations → "Mass hallucination"

- Dimensional rifts → "Localized electromagnetic disturbance"

As he reviewed the system, his phone buzzed with a text from Masters: "Lab results back on latest vic. Nothing in database matches these compounds. What aren't you telling me?"

Ethan glanced at his template, already formulating a response that would satisfy human inquiry while protecting supernatural secrets. The art of hidden truth had become his specialty - maintaining justice in both worlds through careful documentation and strategic silence.

His system was evolving with each case, becoming more sophisticated as synthetic supernatural crimes forced him to bridge increasingly complex gaps between human law and supernatural justice. The template wasn't just about protecting secrets anymore - it was about creating a framework where both forms of law could coexist, serving justice while preserving necessary boundaries.

He began composing his response to Masters, each word carefully chosen to maintain both truths and necessary illusions. In Daybridge's shadowed reality, effective law enforcement meant mastering the delicate balance between revelation and concealment, between human justice and supernatural necessity.

His phone lit up with responses to this approach:

Diana: "Pack approves hybrid investigation model. Sets sustainable precedent."

Masters: "Following corporate conspiracy angle. Things finally making sense."

Reynolds: "Investigation methods unusual but producing results."

The downtown killing became a turning point. Not choosing between worlds but finding ways to serve both effectively. Each piece of evidence carefully filtered through appropriate channels:

Corporate financial records revealed synthetic compound production (Human)

Vampire feeding violations documented through supernatural courts (Supernatural)

Chemical analysis exposed illegal drug trials (Human)

Magic traces contained by witch covens (Supernatural)

"Impressive work," Reynolds admitted, reviewing his final report. "Unorthodox methods, but solid evidence chain."

Because the evidence had been carefully curated to tell necessary truths to both worlds. The human investigation revealed corporate crimes. The supernatural investigation addressed vampire violations. Each discovery strengthened rather than exposed the other.

His phone delivered final confirmation:

Viktor Blackwood: "Council accepts hybrid jurisdiction model. New precedent established."

Marina: "Synthetic compound production facility located through police investigation."

Diana: "Pack territories secured through official channels."

The scrutiny hadn't diminished, but he'd proven it was possible to satisfy both systems of justice. Not by choosing between them, but by understanding how they could complement each other.

Rodriguez dropped another file on his desk. "New case. More weird blood work. Still watching how you handle these, Reeves."

Let them watch. He'd shown that maintaining cover didn't mean choosing sides. It meant building bridges between worlds while preserving necessary boundaries. Each case would reinforce that balance, proving that one detective could serve both human law and supernatural justice.

His phone lit up one last time. Masters: "Whatever you're involved in, it's making a difference. Just be careful. Department's still watching."

Time to prove again that impossible cases could have possible solutions - even under the watchful eyes of those who served only one world while he walked between both.

CHAPTER ELEVEN

THE GATHERING STORM

THE ENCOUNTER CAME during what should have been a routine patrol. Ethan's enhanced senses detected them first - werewolves whose scents were wrong, synthetic markers tainting natural pack signatures. They emerged from the shadows near Kane Industries: six figures moving with unnaturally synchronized precision.

"Detective Reeves," their leader stepped forward, his movements mechanical despite their fluidity."We've been expecting you."

The wrongness hit Ethan's supernatural instincts like a physical blow. Their pack bonds felt artificial, programmed rather than organic. Even their wolf aspects seemed manufactured, lacking the wild essence that marked true werewolves.

The fight revealed their true nature. They moved like combat units, each action precisely coordinated. But they couldn't adapt when Ethan's natural wolf instincts disrupted their patterns. Their enhancement gave them strength but cost them improvisation.

"Impressive programming," Ethan noted, analyzing their combat algorithms. "But real wolves don't fight like machines."

His phone buzzed during the confrontation:

Marina: "Chemical analysis confirms synthetic markers rewrite supernatural DNA."

Viktor Blackwood: "Similar patterns in vampire attacks. Artificial blood bonds."

Claudia: "They're not just copying supernatural abilities - they're industrializing them."

The encounter provided crucial intelligence: The synthetic infiltrators weren't just enhanced humans - they were attempts to mass-produce supernatural abilities. Each faction's unique powers are reduced to programmable formulas.

At the Blackwood mansion gathering, Ethan presented his findings:

"They're not targeting individual factions," he explained. "They're deconstructing supernatural society itself. Breaking down what makes each group unique into synthetic components."

Evidence spread across ancient tables:

Vampire feeding patterns reduced to chemical formulas

Werewolf pack dynamics mapped into algorithms

Fae glamours analyzed as programmable frequencies

"Look at your conflicts," Ethan continued. "Each fight weakens supernatural bonds while strengthening synthetic alternatives. They're not just infiltrating - they're replacing."

His phone supported the pattern:

Diana: "Synthetic enhanced wolves challenging pack hierarchies."

Xavier: "Artificial blood bonds corrupting vampire houses."

Lady Moonweaver: "Fae energies being mechanically replicated."

～

CHAPTER TWELVE

SYSTEMATIC EROSION

IN THE DEPTHS of The Crimson Cellar's war room, Ethan laid out his evidence before the gathered supernatural leaders. Crime scene photos, chemical analyses, and behavioral studies covered the ancient oak table, each piece revealing part of a terrifying pattern.

"Look at the progression," he said, arranging the documents chronologically. "Each synthetic advancement targets a specific supernatural trait, then moves to exploit the resulting weakness."

Viktor Blackwood studied the vampire data with growing concern. "The synthetic blood compounds don't just mimic our nutritional needs - they create chemical dependencies that override natural feeding instincts. Three covens have already reported members unable to process natural blood after exposure."

Diana Kane spread out reports from affected werewolf packs. "The synthetic markers are becoming more sophisticated. They don't just mask scent - they actively rewrite pack recognition. Wolves exposed to these compounds show decreased ability to recognize legitimate pack bonds."

"It's worse for the fae," Eleanor Thorne added, her ageless features tight with worry. "The synthetic energies are corrupting our ancient ley lines. Each artificial signature weakens the natural boundaries between realms. We've lost contact with three minor courts already."

Ethan moved to a digital display showing attack patterns across Daybridge:

SYNTHETIC INFILTRATION ANALYSIS

Vampire Targets:

- Blood supply chains contaminated with synthetic additives

- Thrall bonds weakened by chemical interference

- Hierarchy disrupted by artificial loyalties

- Feeding grounds compromised by synthetic alternatives

Werewolf Vulnerabilities:

- Pack recognition altered by synthetic markers

- Territory boundaries confused by artificial signatures

- Natural instincts suppressed by chemical conditioning

- Alpha authority undermined by programmed responses

Fae Weaknesses:

- Magical energies diluted by synthetic frequencies

- Realm boundaries destabilized by artificial signatures

- Court hierarchies disrupted by synthetic influence

- Ancient powers replicated through technological means

"The strategy is elegant in its cruelty," Marina James observed, examining financial data. "Each synthetic advancement forces us to adapt, but adaptation only makes us more vulnerable to the next phase.

They're not just replacing us - they're making us participate in our own obsolescence."

Ash's intelligence reports revealed the broader pattern. Supernatural conflicts had increased 300% since the synthetic compounds appeared. Each skirmish provided valuable data for refining the artificial replacements.

"Consider the psychological impact," Claudia added. "Vampires questioning their blood bonds. Wolves doubting pack loyalties. Fae losing confidence in their ancient powers. The synthetic threat isn't just attacking our abilities - it's eroding our identities."

Security footage showed supernatural beings behaving erratically after exposure to synthetic compounds. Vampires breaking traditional feeding protocols. Werewolves ignoring pack hierarchies. Fae unable to access their natural abilities.

"They've weaponized our adaptation instinct," Viktor realized. "Each time we evolve to resist one synthetic threat, we become more susceptible to the next. Our very survival mechanisms are being used against us."

Diana pulled up genetic analyses showing how synthetic compounds integrated with supernatural biology: "The changes become permanent after sufficient exposure. They're not just replacing us - they're transforming us into hybrid beings that depend on their synthetic compounds."

"And while we fight these internal battles," Ethan concluded, "they perfect their synthetic alternatives. Each supernatural conflict provides cover for introducing more artificial elements into our communities."

The evidence painted a devastating picture - a systematic campaign to undermine and replace supernatural society from within. The synthetic threat wasn't just about creating artificial supernatural beings - it was about making natural ones obsolete.

"We've been fighting the wrong war," Eleanor said quietly. "These local conflicts, these territorial disputes - they're all distractions from the real threat. They don't need to destroy us if they can simply make us irrelevant."

As the council absorbed these implications, Ethan's phone buzzed with another crime scene alert. But now they understood - each supernatural death, each faction conflict, each territorial dispute was another data point for those seeking to perfect synthetic replacement.

The question wasn't just how to stop the immediate threats, but how to preserve the essential nature of supernatural society against an enemy that turned adaptation itself into a weapon. Somewhere in Daybridge, the architects of this synthetic evolution watched their plan unfold, while the very beings they sought to replace fought battles that only hastened their own obsolescence.

CHAPTER THIRTEEN
PERFECT STORM

IN KANE TOWER's secure conference room, Ethan played the security footage again. The figure moved with impossible fluidity - leaping with werewolf strength, vanishing at vampire speed, wielding fae energies that shouldn't coexist in one being. The implications were staggering.

"Dr. Helena Winters," Marina said, bringing up personnel files on the main display. "PhD in Xenobiology from MIT. Masters in Biochemical Engineering. Recruited by Kane Industries' Special Research Division in 2020."

The profile painted a picture of brilliant obsession:

PERSONNEL FILE: DR. HELENA WINTERS

Research Focus: Cross-species genetic adaptation

Key Projects:

- Supernatural genetic mapping

- Biomolecular enhancement

- Adaptive DNA reconstruction

Status: Terminated (2018) - Ethical violations

WARNING: Subject displayed increasing instability

- Unauthorized human trials

- Restricted materials theft

- Classified data breach

"She wasn't fired," Diana corrected, accessing sealed records. "She evolved beyond our control. The termination was cover for her transformation. She became her own experiment."

Evidence streamed in from multiple sources:

From Masters:

"DOD contracts under shell company 'Evolution Dynamics' - $50M black budget funding. Classified status: UMBRA."

From Reynolds:

"Multiple shell corporations traced to offshore accounts. Pattern suggests systematic resource acquisition for large-scale production."

From Eleanor:

"Magical disturbances showing organized testing pattern. Synthetic signatures becoming more sophisticated."

Ethan compiled the data on secure servers:

SYNTHETIC EVOLUTION ANALYSIS

Phase 1: Individual Enhancement

- Vampire abilities synthesized

- Werewolf traits replicated

- Fae powers artificially induced

. . .

Phase 2: Hybrid Development

- Multiple supernatural aspects combined

- Stability issues resolved

- Natural limitations removed

Phase 3: Species Engineering

- New genetic template created

- Traditional weaknesses eliminated

- Enhanced capabilities standardized

Current Status: Advanced Integration

- Synthetic beings showing evolved abilities

- Multiple supernatural aspects manifesting

- Traditional limitations overcome

Diana's analysis of recovered lab data revealed the true scope: "She's not just creating enhanced individuals - she's engineering an entirely new species. One that combines all supernatural abilities without our evolutionary limitations."

The evidence painted a chilling picture of methodical advancement:

EVOLUTIONARY PROGRESSION

Stage 1: Basic Synthesis

- Individual supernatural traits replicated

- Limited stability achieved

- Significant side effects

.   .   .

Stage 2: Trait Combination

- Multiple abilities merged

- Increased stability

- Reduced limitations

Stage 3: Complete Integration

- Full supernatural spectrum accessed

- Perfect stability achieved

- Natural limitations removed

Final Goal: New Species

- Supernatural abilities fully combined

- Traditional weaknesses eliminated

- Enhanced capabilities standardized

Then Ethan's phone lit up with a message from the architect herself:

"Impressive analysis, Detective. You understand the pattern but not the purpose. This isn't destruction - it's transcendence. Care to discuss evolution in person?"

The supernatural leaders exchanged glances as implications sank in. Their ancient societies faced replacement by beings that combined all their strengths with none of their weaknesses.

Viktor's voice carried centuries of concern: "She's not just threatening our existence - she's offering to make us obsolete."

Another message arrived:

· · ·

"Your position is unique, Detective. A human who successfully bridged supernatural transformation. You could help guide this evolution. Or be replaced by it. Choose carefully."

Diana studied tactical displays showing supernatural activity across Daybridge: "She's forcing confrontation. Making us reveal our capabilities through conflict."

"Every fight provides more data," Eleanor added. "Each supernatural clash helps perfect her synthetic species."

The final pieces aligned into terrible clarity - they weren't just fighting synthetic replacements but participating in their own evolutionary obsolescence. Each supernatural conflict refined Dr. Winters's formulas, bringing her closer to engineering their successors.

Ethan's phone delivered her final message of the night:

"The storm's already here, Detective. The only choice is whether to rise above it or be washed away. Shall we discuss the future of both our species?"

The supernatural leaders united around a common threat; ancient enmities set aside before the prospect of systematic replacement. But Dr. Winters' invitation suggested this was more than a battle for survival - it was a confrontation over the future of supernatural evolution itself.

As the meeting ended, new alliances formed between age-old rivals. Vampire houses, werewolf packs, and fae courts prepared to face an enemy that threatened not just their lives, but their very essence. At the center stood a detective who had shown them the true cost of division, now facing his own choice between guiding evolution or being consumed by it.

The synthetic storm gathered strength, but supernatural society would meet it united, finally understanding their true enemy. The question wasn't just whether they could survive, but whether ancient powers combined could overcome synthetic evolution, or if Dr. Winters's new species would inherit both worlds.

CHAPTER FOURTEEN

RED RIVER RISING

THE TIP CAME from Marina at 3 AM: massive energy fluctuations at Red River Pharmaceuticals' restricted research wing. By the time Ethan arrived, supernatural factions were already converging on the facility. The Kane pack led the charge, with Diana's elite warriors taking point. The MacGregor vampire coven moved through shadows, their blood-hunters tracking synthetic signatures. Lady Moonweaver's fae scouts shimmered at the perimeter, their ancient magic detecting unnatural energies.

Through the reinforced glass, Ethan witnessed the aftermath of Dr. Winters' latest experiment: Red River researchers convulsing as forced transformations tore through their bodies. Their partially enhanced forms caught between human and wolf, synthetic pack bonds burning through natural limitations.

The horror unfolded across three levels of sterile laboratories. In Lab 7, three bodies lay twisted by failed enhancement, their forms grotesque parodies of supernatural transformation. Research notes scattered across blood-stained floors revealed Dr. Winters' ambition - the systematic deconstruction of supernatural genetics into replicable formulas.

Lab 12 held live subjects strapped to medical tables, monitoring equipment recording their forced transformations. Their screams carried both human agony and wolf rage as synthetic markers rewrote their DNA. In Lab 16, Dr. Winters' private research station displayed the project's scope through holographic models - supernatural abilities reduced to chemical equations and binary code.

"Fascinating timing, Detective," Dr. Winters' voice echoed through the facility's speakers. "You're about to witness the next stage of supernatural evolution."

The Kane pack moved with practiced precision. Diana's warriors split into traditional hunting formations, their natural pack bonds allowing seamless coordination. Beta teams secured the perimeter while Alpha strike forces targeted enhanced subjects. Centuries of pack warfare experience proved decisive against synthetic combat protocols.

The MacGregor coven's blood-hunters traced synthetic markers through the facility's ventilation system, neutralizing airborne compounds. Their ancient blood magic countered chemical enhancers, preventing further forced transformations. Lady Moonweaver's fae maintained magical containment, their glamours keeping human authorities from witnessing supernatural warfare.

The facility's lower levels revealed the project's true scope. Holding cells contained dozens of test subjects in various stages of enhancement. The data center processed supernatural genetic codes into programmable sequences. In the central lab, Dr. Winters' synthetic transformation chamber stood ready to create enhanced beings with multiple supernatural attributes.

"The future isn't natural selection," Dr. Winters explained through facility feeds. "It's directed evolution. Supernatural power without supernatural limitations."

The crisis peaked as the full moon rose. Enhanced subjects broke containment, their synthetic powers growing stronger even as their bodies began breaking down. But as lunar energy flooded the facility, their artificial pack bonds shattered. Synthetic enhancement couldn't replicate the primal connection between wolf and moon.

Diana led the Kane pack's final assault personally. Her warriors moved with fluid grace born from true supernatural heritage. Enhanced subjects fell before coordinated pack tactics, their programmed combat patterns failing against natural wolf instincts. The MacGregor blood-hunters purged synthetic compounds while fae magic contained the chaos.

The data breach's consequences would echo through both worlds. Federal agencies seized terabytes of supernatural research, requiring massive containment efforts. Vampire houses discovered their blood bond secrets compromised. Werewolf packs faced exposure of ancient transformation rites. The fae courts found their glamor frequencies mapped into reproducible patterns.

Supernatural society adapted. The Kane pack established new security protocols, incorporating lessons from synthetic enhancement attempts. Vampire houses enhanced their blood magic defenses. Fae courts layered their glamours with additional complexity. But the funda-mental breach couldn't be undone - supernatural genetics had been systematically analyzed, creating templates for future synthetic experiments.

The facility's containment failed completely as dawn approached. Diana's pack secured surviving test subjects while vampire blood-hunters eliminated synthetic compounds. Fae magic erased evidence of supernatural warfare, leaving a scene human authorities could process.

Dr. Winters escaped in the chaos, but her voice carried through final facility broadcasts: "Fascinating data, Detective. But only a setback. We'll perfect the formula eventually."

The Red River incident ended with changed realities. The Kane pack's authority grew through their decisive action. Supernatural factions developed new alliances against synthetic threats. Human authorities gained carefully controlled glimpses of powers beyond their understanding.

Time to document it all - in police reports that explained what could be explained, and supernatural records that preserved what had to remain hidden. The incident had tested both worlds. Now to build stronger bridges between them while maintaining necessary boundaries.

The data breach's longest-lasting impact might be psychological. Supernatural beings faced the reality that their most fundamental attributes could be studied, mapped, and potentially replicated. The Kane pack led efforts to strengthen natural bonds, proving genuine supernatural connections trumped synthetic enhancement. But the knowledge that such enhancement was possible changed everything.

Dawn revealed a facility in ruins, its laboratories destroyed by supernatural warfare. But the real damage was to computers and backup drives - supernatural secrets reduced to data, waiting to be exploited by the next researcher willing to push evolution's boundaries. The incident had ended, but its consequences would shape both worlds for years to come.

CHAPTER FIFTEEN

SHADOWS AND SYNTHETICS

DR. WINTERS' escape route revealed careful planning born from years of contingency preparation. As supernatural forces breached Red River's upper levels, she activated Protocol Omega - a cascade of system failures that transformed the facility's secure sublevel into her extraction corridor.

Through surveillance feeds, Ethan tracked her methodical retreat. She moved with unnatural fluidity, her form shifting between supernatural aspects. Vampire speed carried her through security checkpoints. Werewolf strength tore through containment doors. Fae glamour confused pursuit teams.

"Evolution demands sacrifice," her final facility broadcast echoed as she reached the maintenance tunnels. Behind her, experimental subjects convulsed in their cells - living distractions to cover her escape.

The tunnel network revealed her long-term strategy. Each junction contained cached supplies: synthetic compounds, research backups, identity documents. She'd prepared this exit route while building Red River's research empire, embedding escape paths within legitimate construction.

Marina's analysis tracked her movement through Daybridge's underground infrastructure:

"Multiple synthetic signatures detected in maintenance shaft 23B... Energy fluctuations consistent with enhanced capabilities... Chemical traces showing evolutionary adaptations..."

Dr. Winters emerged in three locations simultaneously - each instance displaying different supernatural attributes. Security cameras caught glimpses: a vampire's grace in the financial district, wolf reflexes near the industrial zone, fae glamour by the river docks. Each sighting triggered different pursuit teams, dividing supernatural forces.

The truth surfaced in analyzed patterns. She'd developed a way to project synthetic duplicates, each embodying specific enhanced traits. The real Dr. Winters used the confusion to access a hidden facility beneath an abandoned Kane Industries subsidiary.

Within weeks, her activities rippled through both worlds. Shell companies purchased specialized equipment. Research facilities reported missing classified data. Test subjects disappeared from supernatural custody. Each action built toward something larger.

Her synthetic presence grew more sophisticated. Enhanced infiltrators appeared in corporate boards, supernatural gatherings, and government agencies. Each carried carefully modified markers - improvements on Red River's original formulas.

Messages reached Ethan through encrypted channels:

"Natural selection is too slow, Detective. Evolution needs guidance. Red River was just the prototype. Watch true synthetic advancement emerge."

Investigation revealed her new operation's scope. Multiple research sites, each studying different aspects of supernatural genetics. Artificial pack structures testing enhanced wolf dynamics. Synthetic blood bonds examining vampire hierarchies. Manufactured glamours probing fae limitations.

Most disturbing were reports of willing test subjects - supernatural beings volunteering for enhancement. They emerged transformed, carrying hybrid abilities that defied traditional limitations. A werewolf displaying vampire speed. A vampire wielding fae glamour. Each success advancing Dr. Winters' synthetic evolution.

Her pattern suggested a larger design. Red River's public failure masked private progress. Each enhanced subject provided data for more sophisticated synthetics. Every supernatural response revealed new adaptation opportunities.

Marina's analysis confirmed the progression: "Synthetic markers showing generational improvement. Each iteration more stable than previous versions. She's building something bigger than Red River ever was."

Dr. Winters' activities painted a clear picture: Red River wasn't her main operation - it was a proof of concept. Her real work continued in scattered facilities, each advancing different aspects of supernatural enhancement. The public facility's destruction covered the growth of something far more sophisticated.

Her final message carried both invitation and warning: "You can't stop evolution, Detective. But you could help guide it. Natural and synthetic powers in careful balance. Consider the possibilities before choosing sides."

The threat had evolved beyond a single facility. Dr. Winters' escape seeded synthetic advancement throughout both worlds. Now her work continued in shadows, improving formulas and gathering willing subjects. Each enhancement brought her closer to her goal: to guide supernatural evolution through synthetic means.

The hunt continued, but the game had changed. No longer containing a single threat but tracking an evolving synthetic presence. Dr. Winters' escape marked the beginning of a longer battle - one that would test both natural supernatural powers and their artificial counterparts.

Time would reveal which proved stronger: traditional supernatural bonds or synthetic enhancement. But Dr. Winters' activities suggested she already knew the answer. She wasn't just escaping - she was advancing to the next phase of her evolutionary design.

The real question was how many others would choose synthetic enhancement over natural supernatural power. Each willing subject strengthened her position. Every successful enhancement validated her vision. Dr. Winters hadn't just escaped - she'd expanded her operation beyond conventional containment.

Now supernatural society faced a more insidious threat: the temptation of engineered evolution. Dr. Winters offered power without traditional limitations. Her escape ensured that choice would continue spreading through both worlds, testing fundamental supernatural bonds against synthetic advancement.

❧

CHAPTER SIXTEEN

CHAPTER SIXTEEN
FULL MOON RISING

THE POLITICAL AFTERSHOCKS of the Red River incident rippled through both worlds. Mayor Smith called an emergency press conference announcing the successful containment of a coordinated terrorist attack on a pharmaceutical research facility. Behind closed doors, a more complex story unfolded at the supernatural summit within Blackwood mansion's ancient walls.

Representatives from every major pack gathered to address the crisis. Red River survivors, stripped of synthetic enhancement, sought reintegration into traditional pack structures. Kane territory had expanded by right of conquest, while ancient laws demanded response to the corruption of pack bonds.

Xavier Thorne's observation cut through the heated territorial debates: "The balance of power has shifted. Red River's synthetic experiment failed, but other packs watched closely."

The political landscape transformed on multiple fronts. Federal investigators descended upon Red River Pharmaceuticals while corporate board members faced criminal charges. Military contracts underwent intense scrutiny as intelligence agencies examined synthetic research programs. Within supernatural circles, pack territories underwent major redistribution as former Red River wolves sought new allegiances.

Marina reported three smaller packs requesting Kane protection. Viktor Blackwood tracked vampire houses reorganizing their wolf alliances. Eleanor detected witch covens monitoring the restructuring of pack bonds across the city.

The most significant change emerged in pack dynamics. Ethan's actions during the full moon crisis shattered traditional models of rigid territories and isolated pack justice. In their place arose flexible agreements and strategic alliances. Diana recognized the unprecedented nature of his achievement: packs working with human authorities while maintaining supernatural autonomy.

The political realignment manifested in stages. Red River survivors found homes in accepting packs while synthetic research facilities shut down. Pack territories stabilized under new agreements as human authorities contained exposure. This led to established cooperation protocols, joint security measures, and hybrid justice systems bridging both worlds.

The supernatural summit formalized these changes through new pack laws. Hybrid authority positions gained recognition alongside protocols for supernatural-human cooperation. The council established guidelines for flexible territories and standards for integrating former synthetic-enhanced wolves.

Diana's announcement marked a crucial shift: "Your position is now officially recognized - Mediator between packs, bridge between worlds." Most significantly, this new role carried independence from traditional pack obligations. As Mediator, Ethan could maintain neutrality while serving both supernatural and human interests.

Former Red River wolves provided vital perspective on this evolution. "The artificial pack bonds felt empty," one testified. "Like connections without meaning. Real pack bonds grow from choice and trust." This understanding reshaped pack politics from forced loyalty to earned respect, from isolated power to strategic alliance.

The transformation extended to human relations. Supernatural society began viewing human authorities as potential allies rather than threats to avoid. Ethan's position proved that secrets could be maintained while fostering selective cooperation.

Captain Reynolds confirmed the success: "Whatever you're doing with inter-department cooperation, it's working." Diana's formal recognition of Mediator status established precedent for future supernatural-human bridges.

The Red River incident had destroyed synthetic enhancement through artificial bonds but created something more valuable: natural evolution through strategic cooperation and flexible authority. Each crisis would test these new relationships, proving whether supernatural society could maintain traditional strengths while adapting to modern realities.

As the full moon set on old pack politics, it rose on new possibilities. Ethan's independent Mediator position became more than unique - it established a template for future supernatural-human cooperation. His freedom from pack obligations allowed him to serve both worlds with true neutrality, maintaining balance between ancient traditions and necessary change.

Diana's final message captured the moment's weight: "You've changed how packs relate to each other and the human world. Now we see if these changes survive the next storm." The challenge ahead lay in proving this new model could withstand whatever gathered on the horizon, while Ethan's independence ensured decisions would serve both worlds' best interests rather than any single pack's agenda.

CHAPTER SEVENTEEN

BETWEEN MOONS

ETHAN SAT AT HIS DESK, the midnight shift quiet except for the gentle hum of fluorescent lights. His fingers traced the worn edges of case files - some officially closed, others still haunting the shadows between human law and supernatural justice.

Three years had passed since that first full moon transformation in Kane territory. The badge on his desk reflected both worlds now: Detective Ethan Reeves, officially assigned to Special Investigations, unofficially recognized as a supernatural Mediator. His phone buzzed with messages from both realms - Marina's supernatural updates alongside Reynolds' precinct reports.

Opening his bottom drawer, he pulled out a leather-bound journal. Diana had given it to him after the Red River incident, suggesting he document the cases that shaped his unique position. "History needs witnesses," she'd said, "especially when it bridges two worlds."

The journal's first entries captured his stumbling introduction to supernatural society - learning to control transformations while investigating mysterious deaths. Those early cases taught him to balance human law with pack justice, each investigation building trust between worlds.

Now, as an independent Mediator, those past cases took on new significance. Each one had contributed to his current position, teaching lessons about navigating between human authority and supernatural power. The evidence boxes in storage held more than just solved crimes - they marked steps in his evolution from confused new werewolf to respected bridge between worlds.

His fingers paused on a particular file: The Riverward Murders. That case had first revealed the vampire houses' influence in city politics. The MacGregor coven still maintained careful alliance after his handling of their internal justice. Before that had been the Dockside Disappearances, where fae glamour concealed a deeper conspiracy.

Each investigation had added layers to his understanding. The Warehouse District killings exposed how witch covens regulated magical commerce. The Eastside Hauntings revealed ghost territories overlapping mortal boundaries. The Market Street incident proved that werewolf packs could cooperate with human authorities.

A photo slipped from between reports - his first crime scene after transformation. How naive he'd been then, trying to explain supernatural evidence through standard police procedure. Now he moved smoothly between explanations, crafting reports that satisfied human oversight while preserving necessary secrets.

His phone lit up with a new message. Captain Morris requesting his presence at a fresh crime scene. The details suggested another case straddling both worlds - human victims, supernatural signatures. Time to put those hard-earned lessons to work.

Standing, Ethan gathered his badge and gun. The journal went back in its drawer, past cases filed but not forgotten. Each one had shaped his path from confused rookie to respected Mediator. Now those experiences would guide him through whatever waited in the darkness ahead.

The precinct doors opened to a waning moon. Somewhere in the city, human crime scene techs were preserving evidence while supernatural sensors detected magical traces. Another case bridging both worlds. Another chance to prove cooperation could triumph over conflict.

His phone buzzed again - Marina warning of unusual energy signatures, Viktor Blackwood reporting vampire interest, Eleanor detecting witch involvement. The past three years had taught him to weave these threads together, finding truth in the space between natural and supernatural law.

Time to add another chapter to that leather-bound journal. But first, a crime scene waited. Another mystery stretching across both his worlds. Another chance to prove his unique position served both human justice and supernatural order.

Ethan walked into the night, carrying lessons from past cases toward whatever challenges waited ahead. The moon watched his progress, no longer a threatening force but a familiar companion. He'd learned to navigate by its light, finding paths between worlds that others couldn't see.

His car turned toward the reported crime scene. Behind him, the precinct held files documenting his journey from newly turned werewolf to independent Mediator. Ahead lie fresh mysteries needing that hard-earned experience. Time to prove past lessons could illuminate present darkness.

In his pocket, his phone continued collecting messages from both worlds. Each one represented connections forged through past investigations. Each one confirmed his unique position bridging supernatural and human justice. Now to apply those relationships to whatever waited at the end of this night's drive.

PART TWO: PRESENT DAY

CHAPTER EIGHTEEN

THE WAREHOUSE DISTRICT MURDERS

THE FIRST BODY appeared in Container 247B, sealed from the inside. No signs of forced entry, no blood despite precise surgical incisions. Ellen Torres, shipping coordinator, found slumped against steel walls that held no fingerprints, no trace evidence, nothing to explain how she got there.

"Impossible," Masters muttered, reviewing security footage. "Container was sealed in Singapore, arrived unopened."

Ethan's enhanced senses told a different story. Beneath industrial cleaner and sea salt, he caught the distinctive sweetness of vampire feeding. Not the controlled precision of house-sanctioned hunting, but something feral, desperate.

The second victim surfaced three weeks later. Michael Cole, customs inspector, locked inside Container 389C. Same surgical precision, same bloodless scene, same impossible circumstances. The human investigation focused on medical personnel with port access, but Ethan recognized the pattern.

His phone buzzed with a message from Viktor Blackwood: "Mac-

Gregor house concerned about unauthorized feeding. Requesting discreet inquiry."

The vampire houses maintained strict feeding protocols - willing donors, controlled amounts, no deaths. This rogue behavior threatened centuries of careful balance. But explaining that to Captain Morris would be problematic.

Marina's analysis arrived encrypted: "Feeding patterns show excessive blood extraction - 1.8 times normal vampire consumption. Tissue damage indicates frenzied state. Supernatural markers in victim's blood show corrupted turning attempt - perpetrator likely unstable, possibly newly turned without proper house guidance."

Masters detective instincts picked up subtle inconsistencies. "Medical examiner's stumped," he reported. "No blood pooling, no spatter patterns. Bodies completely drained but no evidence of where the blood went. And these incisions - too precise for rage kills but positioned all wrong for organ harvesting."

Ethan recognized his partner's tone. Masters might not know about supernatural elements, but years of investigation had honed his instincts. His suspicion of deeper mysteries meant tighter scrutiny of evidence, making it harder to maintain supernatural secrecy.

Shipping manifests revealed Dragon Crown Shipping's CEO, Michael Drake, presenting perfect cooperation while setting off every supernatural warning signal Ethan possessed. Marina's follow-up analysis confirmed: "Residual energy signatures in containers match unregistered vampire presence. Recent turning, no house control markers, signs of deteriorating control."

Late-night surveillance revealed Drake's true nature. The CEO moved with inhuman grace through secure areas, selecting victims with predatory precision. Security chief Alan Powell provided access codes and cleanup, believing he served a simple smuggling operation.

"Complicated," Viktor Blackwood commented when Ethan reported his findings." Drake's turned without house sanction. MacGregors want internal justice."

The third victim never made it to a container. Ethan's enhanced hearing caught the struggle in Drake's office. He arrived to find the CEO feeding on a young clerk, Powell standing guard outside.

The fight destroyed three offices and a conference room. Drake's feral strength matched Ethan's werewolf abilities, but lack of house training left him vulnerable to supernatural combat experience. Powell fled but triggered no alarms - human authorities wouldn't interrupt vampire justice.

"Interesting technique," observed MacGregor house enforcer Victoria Penner, arriving to witness Drake's submission. "The houses acknowledge your handling of this matter."

The official resolution satisfied both worlds. Powell's arrest closed the human investigation - evidence suggested he killed victims during smuggling operations. Drake faced vampire justice while his company underwent "restructuring." The houses strengthened their oversight while human authorities enhanced port security.

CHAPTER NINETEEN
ECHOES IN BLOOD

THREE MONTHS LATER, Marina's analysis of new victims revealed disturbing differences: "Feeding signatures show controlled extraction but corrupted supernatural markers. Previous victims showed panic feeding - these show methodical harvesting. Blood chemistry indicates ritual purpose rather than sustenance."

Masters' suspicions deepened with each case. His case board connected seemingly unrelated details: shipping schedules, victim backgrounds, trace evidence invisible to supernatural senses. His instincts were building a picture dangerously close to the truth.

"These aren't random kills," he insisted, studying autopsy reports. "The blood removal is too precise, too controlled. Someone's collecting it for something specific."

Marina confirmed his theory from a supernatural perspective: "New killer's markers show house training but corrupted by external influence. Blood contains traces of ritual magic - they're harvesting for specific supernatural purpose."

The investigation became a delicate balance. Masters' methodical detective work threatened to expose supernatural elements, while

Ethan's enhanced senses detected an increasingly complex magical agenda. The new killer wasn't just feeding - they were collecting materials for something bigger.

His phone lit up with Victoria's message: "House MacGregor requests assistance. Previous cooperation noted. Similar discretion required. Ritual elements suggest forbidden practice."

Time to revisit the warehouse district's shadows. But this hunter was learning from Drake's mistakes, evolving beyond simple container kills. The question was whether Ethan could solve the case without exposing supernatural secrets to his increasingly suspicious partner.

Marina's latest analysis raised the stakes: "Ritual traces accumulating in victim's blood. Pattern suggests preparation for major working. Time-sensitive situation."

Masters was already connecting new evidence to old suspicions. "Something about these shipping deaths isn't adding up. Like we only caught part of Drake's operation. These new kills - they're too similar to be coincidence, too different to be the same killer."

Ethan studied crime scene photos, catching magical traces that human investigators would never notice. The warehouse district was about to reveal new secrets, testing his ability to resolve supernatural threats while preserving his cover as a normal detective.

The real challenge would be staying ahead of Masters' investigation. His partner's instincts were too good to ignore the supernatural elements forever. Sooner or later, something would have to give - but for now, there was a magically enhanced killer to catch before they completed whatever ritual they were preparing.

CHAPTER TWENTY

BLOOD RITUALS AND BREAKING POINTS

MARINA'S MIDNIGHT message included detailed architectural renderings of Trinity Warehouse overlaid with supernatural energy readings. The building's seemingly mundane design masked an elaborate magical containment system.

"Trinity Warehouse's three wings form a perfect triquetra," Marina explained. "Each wing aligns with major ley lines - Commerce Line to the north, Ancient Way to the southeast, and the Dark Path to the southwest. The Central Courtyard marks the convergence point where Konstantin was sealed."

The warehouse's true nature revealed itself through its intricate layout. The North Wing rose three stories, each floor's corridors forming runic patterns for binding. In the Southeast Wing, circular chambers connected by spiraling hallways were designed to contain magical energy. The Southwest Wing housed a maze of intersecting corridors creating magical barriers. At the heart, the Central Courtyard's pentagonal shape featured obsidian pillars disguised as support columns. Below it all, an underground network of tunnels formed the final binding circle, hidden beneath shipping storage.

"Elder Konstantin's sealing required incredible power," Marina's analysis continued. Historical records painted a terrifying picture of his abilities. He could control multiple blood-bonded vampires simultaneously and proved immune to traditional vampire weaknesses. Most disturbing was his ability to walk in daylight and corrupt humans without physical contact. His mental domination reached across vast distances, and his manipulation of blood magic remained unmatched in vampire history.

The roles of Succession and Sacrifice carried specific requirements that the killer had been methodically fulfilling. Succession demanded a victim from a bloodline of leadership, taken during their peak of influence - representing the continuation of vampire authority. Marina had identified three potential targets matching these criteria. The Sacrifice requirement proved more complex: the victim needed powerful spiritual or supernatural connection, and their blood had to be willingly given. This suggested the killer had an insider accomplice.

Masters' investigation board unknowingly mapped these elements through victim patterns. "All high-ranking victims were killed during career peaks," he noted, studying the names. "And look at these last few candidates - all from old money families or positions of authority."

Ethan recognized names on Masters' list - descendants of families involved in Konstantin's original sealing. The killer wasn't just following ritual requirements but settling ancient scores.

Marina's historical documents revealed Konstantin's terrifying reach. Before his sealing, he controlled most of Eastern Europe's vampire houses. His blood magic could turn entire villages, creating instant armies. The Great Purge of 1872 required an unprecedented alliance of all major houses, three witch covens, and human monster hunters to bring him down.

Recent modifications to Trinity Warehouse betrayed years of preparation. New shipping equipment had been positioned to amplify magical convergence points. Modern security systems would actually enhance ritual energy. Subtle changes to the interior layout strengthened magical channels, while maintenance tunnels provided access to all major ritual points.

"Someone's been preparing this for years," Marina warned. "The killer modified Trinity Warehouse's containment systems to act as focusing points for resurrection instead of binding."

Masters studied recurring patterns in shipping schedules: "Every major incident lines up with lunar phases. Tomorrow night's dark moon marks a total shipping stoppage in all three wings. Building will be completely empty."

The final pieces of Marina's analysis painted a grim picture. Konstantin's return would shatter modern vampire society. His power over blood bonds could enslave younger vampires. His ability to corrupt at a distance could create a pandemic of turnings. The houses would be forced to either submit to his rule or risk exposure fighting him.

Time was critical. The killer had spent years preparing Trinity Warehouse, positioning victims, and gathering power. Tomorrow night's dark moon would complete the alignment of magical and mundane elements.

Masters traced cargo patterns on his map: "Everything flows toward Trinity Warehouse tomorrow night. Whatever's happening, that's where it ends."

Ethan studied the warehouse plans, noting how each mundane security measure doubled as magical enhancement. The killer had created a perfect bridge between human and supernatural worlds - exactly what they needed to bring back a monster who could destroy both.

Marina's final warning carried centuries of dread: "Konstantin's last words before sealing: 'When I return, both wolves and men will kneel to the true blood.' Whatever you're planning, be careful. This isn't just about stopping a ritual - it's about preventing a war that would expose all supernatural beings."

The warehouse waited in darkness, its true purpose hidden behind shipping manifests and security protocols. Tomorrow night, its corridors would either witness a resurrection that could shatter both worlds, or a last-minute salvation that might expose supernatural secrets to stop an ancient evil.

Masters was already preparing tactical plans, unaware that normal police procedures would be useless against blood magic and vampire lords. Ethan had to find a way to stop the ritual while keeping both worlds separate - or decide which secrets were worth sacrificing to prevent a greater catastrophe.

CHAPTER TWENTY-ONE

CONVERGENCE

THE SUPERNATURAL COMBAT in Trinity Warehouse unfolded with devastating intensity. Ethan's werewolf form moved with primal grace, his enhanced strength meeting Roland's centuries of blood magic expertise. The vampire enforcer wielded crimson strands of power, each drop of harvested blood becoming a lethal weapon.

Roland's magical assault filled the air with deadly shards of crystallized blood, while Diana's chanting reached deafening levels. The CEO's blood flowed through ancient channels, beginning the Succession sacrifice. Ethan dodged a volley of blood spears, their impact leaving deep gouges in the reinforced walls.

Masters, despite his injuries, proved remarkably adaptable. From his position behind an obsidian pillar, he observed Roland's attack patterns and called out warnings to Ethan. "He's channeling power through the floor markings - watch your footwork!"

The tide turned when Masters noticed something crucial. "The pillars - they're conducting the energy. Like a circuit." His tactical mind quickly grasped supernatural logistics. Using his service weapon, he shot out the base of two obsidian columns, disrupting the ritual's power flow.

Roland's fury manifested itself in a massive blood wave that threatened to drown everyone in the chamber. Ethan countered with a primal howl that shattered windows throughout the warehouse. The sound's supernatural resonance disrupted Diana's chanting, breaking her concentration at a critical moment.

The ritual's interruption created a cascading failure. Magical energy rebounded through the warehouse's modified architecture. Roland, still connected to the blood magic network, took the full backlash. The vampire's form began to disintegrate as centuries of borrowed power turned inward.

"Master, forgive me," Roland's final words dissolved into ash as his body crumbled. Diana, seeing the ritual's failure, attempted to escape but was caught in the magical backlash. The surviving victims were freed as the blood magic bonds dissipated.

In the aftermath, Masters sat against a broken pillar, processing everything he'd witnessed. Rather than fear or rejection, he displayed remarkable professional curiosity. "So," he said to Ethan, who had reverted to human form, "this explains why you never wanted to get drinks after work."

The revelation's impact rippled outward. House MacGregor's cleanup team arrived to find Masters calmly documenting supernatural evidence. His methodical police work, even in the face of impossible reality, impressed the vampire authorities.

Marina arrived with House MacGregor's eldest, Lord Cameron. After reviewing Masters's handling of the situation, they made an unprecedented decision. Instead of attempting to suppress his memories, they offered him a new role: official liaison between human law enforcement and supernatural authorities.

"The old ways of absolute secrecy are failing," Lord Cameron acknowledged. "We need humans who can bridge both worlds. Detective Masters has proven himself capable of handling this responsibility."

In the following weeks, carefully selected members of law enforcement were brought into a modified version of the truth. A new joint task force was formed, with Masters and Ethan as its core team. Their mission: to handle cases involving both human and supernatural elements while preventing wider exposure.

The supernatural world's response varied. Traditional vampires opposed any human involvement, while younger houses saw the necessity of adaptation. Werewolf packs, led by Ethan's example, cautiously supported controlled revelation to trusted humans.

Masters's adjustment surprised everyone. He approached supernatural cases with the same methodical thoroughness he applied to regular police work. His tactical experience proved invaluable in developing new protocols for supernatural incidents.

"The world's changing," he told Ethan during a late-night stakeout of suspected vampire activity. "Technology, surveillance, social media - complete secrecy was becoming impossible anyway. Better to control the revelation than have it exposed chaotically."

The averted ritual had unexpected consequences. While preventing Konstantin's return, it revealed weaknesses in traditional supernatural containment. New security measures were implemented, blending modern technology with ancient magic. Masters' suggestions for improving supernatural security earned reluctant respect from vampire houses.

Diana's betrayal led to increased scrutiny of historical families involved in supernatural affairs. Other potential traitors were discovered and neutralized before they could attempt similar rituals. The supernatural world began slowly modernizing its approach to secrecy and security.

Ethan found his role evolving. No longer just a werewolf detective hiding his nature, he became an example of successful human-supernatural cooperation. His partnership with Masters demonstrated how both worlds could work together while maintaining necessary discretion.

The night at Trinity Warehouse marked a turning point. Though Konstantin remained sealed, the incident sparked controlled changes in supernatural society. As Masters and Ethan left the warehouse that night, they knew they'd witnessed not just the end of an ancient threat, but the beginning of a new era in human-supernatural relations.

"You know," Masters said, reviewing their case notes, "next time a suspect has glowing eyes, I'd appreciate a heads-up before the shooting starts."

Ethan smiled, realizing that while the world had changed dramatically, some things - like his partner's dry humor - remained comfortingly constant. The future would bring new challenges, but they'd face them together, bridging two worlds that could no longer remain entirely separate.

CHAPTER TWENTY-TWO

THE GHOST MARKETS

AMBER BRIGHTSIDE'S role as bridge between traditional and progressive witch factions proved more challenging than anticipated. The young witch found herself navigating centuries of entrenched magical politics while pushing for necessary reforms.

"The old covenants aren't just rules," she explained to Ethan during a late-night strategy session. "They're living magic, woven into the fabric of our society. Changing them requires more than just new policies - we have to reshape the magic itself."

Her attempts to modernize witch protocols met fierce resistance from the Traditional Covenant, led by Elder Margaret Blackthorn. "These bonds have protected our secrets for millennia," Blackthorn argued during a stormy Council session. "This girl would have us throw away our heritage for convenience."

The ghost market case had exposed critical weaknesses in supernatural governance. Traditional investigation methods proved too slow to prevent human casualties. Yet the old guard correctly pointed out that faster response times increased exposure risks.

Amber's solution was elegant in its simplicity: adapt existing magical frameworks rather than replace them. She worked with senior witches to modify traditional containment spells, making them compatible with modern law enforcement procedures while maintaining magical security.

The political fallout reshaped supernatural power structures. The Greater Council split into three factions: Traditionalists opposing any change, Progressives pushing for complete modernization, and a new Adaptive faction advocating controlled evolution of supernatural law.

Marina's archives revealed similar historical patterns. "Every few centuries, supernatural society faces these crises," she noted. "The question isn't whether to change, but how to change while maintaining necessary secrets."

The new protocols established by the Council reflected this complex balance. Joint human-supernatural investigations were permitted, but with strict oversight. Supernatural crimes affecting humans received expedited response, while purely supernatural matters remained under traditional jurisdiction.

These changes rippled through the community. Vampire houses adjusted their security to account for modern surveillance. Werewolf packs developed new methods of concealing transformations from security cameras. Witch covens began training members in both magical and mundane investigation techniques.

Amber's position grew increasingly crucial. She became the unofficial liaison between magical and mundane authorities, teaching young witches to navigate both worlds. "We're not abandoning tradition," she would tell her students. "We're ensuring its survival by helping it evolve."

The ghost market's aftermath continued influencing supernatural politics. When similar operations emerged in other cities, the reformed protocols allowed faster response. Human law enforcement, though unaware of the full truth, found their investigations mysteriously more effective when certain procedures were followed.

Ethan watched these changes from a unique perspective. His werewolf nature and police work made him a natural ally in Amber's reforms. Together, they developed new guidelines for supernatural crime scenes - ways to preserve both magical and forensic evidence.

The Traditional Covenant's warnings weren't entirely unfounded. A witch cell in Chicago, attempting to follow the new protocols, accidentally exposed magical activity to civilian witnesses. The incident proved that modernization required careful balance.

Amber's response to this setback demonstrated her growing political acumen. She worked with Elder Blackthorn to create a hybrid containment system, combining traditional magical barriers with modern security technology. This cooperation helped ease tensions between factions.

The long-term effects of these changes became clear over the following months. Supernatural crime rates decreased as improved response times deterred magical criminals. Cooperation between different supernatural groups improved, though old rivalries remained.

Masters' department unknowingly became a test case for the new approach. Cases involving supernatural elements were subtly directed to specific detectives trained to handle them appropriately. Success rates improved while exposure risks remained minimal.

"The old ways had wisdom," Amber reflected during a Council review. "But they were designed for a world without security cameras and DNA testing. We needed to adapt while preserving what matters most."

The ghost market case had initiated a controlled evolution in supernatural society. Traditional powers remained respected but were no longer absolute. Young practitioners like Sarah proved that innovation and tradition could coexist.

Elder Blackthorn, in a surprising shift, eventually supported some reforms. "The young ones proved their point," she admitted privately. "Change is inevitable. Better to guide it than resist it."

These developments created new challenges. As supernatural investigations became more efficient, human authorities began noticing patterns. Maintaining secrecy while improving effectiveness required constant vigilance and adaptation.

Amber's work continued, building bridges between old and new. She established training programs for young witches, teaching them to honor traditional magic while embracing necessary changes. Her success offered hope that supernatural society could evolve without losing its essential nature.

The ghost market had marked more than the end of a criminal enterprise. It became a turning point in supernatural history - the moment when ancient powers acknowledged the need to adapt to modern realities while preserving their fundamental secrets.

CHAPTER TWENTY-THREE
THE UNRESOLVED ECHO

THE CRYSTALLINE SIGNATURE defied conventional magical classification. Where vampire magic left a copper-blood taste and werewolf energy crackled with primal force, this presence manifested as geometric impossibilities - fractal patterns that seemed to exist in more dimensions than reality allowed.

"It's like trying to describe a color that doesn't exist," Ethan explained to Marina. "The magic feels like shattered mirrors, each fragment reflecting a different version of reality. But when you try to focus on any single piece, it shifts into something else."

The signature had unique properties. It degraded surveillance equipment in distinctive ways, creating cascade failures in digital systems. Analog cameras captured prismatic distortions - rainbow-like effects that formed perfect Fibonacci spirals before fading away.

Over the years, similar cases emerged with increasing frequency:

2023: The Amsterdam Incident - An experimental quantum encryption system vanished from a sealed underground facility. Witnesses reported seeing crystalline structures growing from walls moments before losing consciousness. Their memories developed strange gaps, remembering events that couldn't have happened.

2024: The Tokyo Paradox - Three separate research facilities reported simultaneous thefts of specialized equipment. Security footage showed the same person in multiple locations, but facial recognition failed to maintain consistency between frames. The crystalline signature was stronger here, leaving visible traces that resembled four-dimensional frost patterns.

2025: The Chicago Loop - A series of thefts from particle physics laboratories created a pattern that, when mapped, formed a perfect Klein bottle configuration across the city. Each crime scene exhibited stronger manifestations of the signature, with some witnesses reporting temporary ability to perceive extra spatial dimensions.

Masters' perspective underwent subtle but profound changes after the original case. Though unaware of the supernatural elements, his detective's instincts evolved. He developed an uncanny ability to recognize when cases contained impossible elements.

"Some evidence doesn't want to be found," he'd say, reviewing similarly puzzling cases. "The harder you look, the less sense it makes. Like trying to photograph your own eye in a mirror - the act of observation changes what you're observing."

His case notes became increasingly philosophical. Standard police methodology gave way to intuitive leaps that somehow aligned with supernatural realities he couldn't consciously perceive. Other detectives started consulting him on "weird cases" - those that seemed to defy normal investigation.

The crystalline signature evolved too. Each new occurrence showed greater complexity, as if the force behind it was learning, adapting. Recent cases exhibited new properties:

Evidence didn't simply vanish; it transformed, becoming something that technically existed but couldn't be meaningfully documented or described

Witnesses retained memories but found them impossible to verbalize, describing them instead through abstract drawings that formed recurring geometric patterns

Digital systems near crime scenes began exhibiting quantum behavior, processing information in ways that violated standard computing logic

"The original thefts weren't just crimes," Marina theorized during a recent consultation. "They were experiments. Whatever force we encountered was testing reality's boundaries. Now it's implementing what it learned."

Ethan's supernatural contacts reported similar patterns globally. The fae courts admitted detecting crystalline signatures at sites of significant technological advancement. These locations formed complex geometric networks when mapped, suggesting coordinated purpose rather than random activity.

Each new case added layers to the mystery:

The Stanford Recursion (2024): A quantum computing laboratory reported equipment rearranging itself into impossible configurations overnight. The crystalline signature here showed signs of deliberate communication - patterns that almost formed comprehensible symbols before shifting into higher-dimensional structures.

The Montreal Metamorphosis (2025): An artificial intelligence research facility experienced localized reality fluctuations. For forty-eight hours, the building existed in multiple quantum states simultaneously. The crystalline signature manifested physically, growing geometric structures that defied Euclidean geometry.

The Berlin Breach (2025): Multiple research institutions reported synchronized anomalies in space-time measurements. The crystalline signature appeared in background radiation readings worldwide, forming patterns that suggested coordinated activity on a global scale.

Masters' response to these later cases revealed his evolved perspective. Though he filed standard reports, his private notes showed deeper insight:

"These aren't normal crimes," he wrote after the Berlin incident. "We're not dealing with theft in any conventional sense. Something is gathering pieces for a puzzle we can't see, using methods we can't understand, for purposes we might not survive knowing."

The recurring cases formed a pattern suggesting escalation. Each new incident pushed further beyond conventional reality. The crystalline signature grew stronger, more complex, more purposeful. What began as seemingly impossible thefts had become something else - perhaps the early stages of a fundamental transformation in reality itself.

Ethan's current case files included a disturbing observation: the time between incidents was decreasing while their impact increased. Recent manifestations of the crystalline signature showed signs of consciousness, as if the force behind them was becoming aware of being observed.

"We're not investigating crimes anymore," he noted in his personal records. "We're documenting the emergence of something new. The question isn't who's responsible - it's what are they becoming, and what does that mean for both human and supernatural reality?"

The Unresolved Echo had evolved from a mystery into a harbinger. Each new case added evidence that reality itself was being systematically reconstructed, one impossible theft at a time. The crystalline signature wasn't just a magical trace - it was the fingerprint of something rewriting the rules of existence.

CHAPTER TWENTY-FOUR
THE PACK KILLER

AFTER WALSH'S CAPTURE, pack security underwent a radical transformation. The North American Pack Council (PAC) established the first comprehensive modern security protocols, codified in what became known as the Walsh Protocols.

"We can't just rely on shadows anymore," Alpha Regina explained during the continental pack summit. "Modern threats require modern countermeasures."

The new security framework transformed how packs operated in the digital age. Pack members now receive intensive training in maintaining consistent human identities that could withstand deep background checks. Regular sweeps for electronic monitoring became standard practice, while coordinated pack movements were designed to avoid pattern recognition. Emergency response protocols established predetermined cover stories and evidence management procedures for supernatural incidents.

Masters' evolution following the Walsh case proved both subtle and significant. His investigative instincts began picking up patterns he couldn't consciously explain. He developed an uncanny ability to sense when cases had supernatural elements, though he rationalized these insights through conventional logic.

"Some cases feel different," he told Ethan during a late-night review of cold files. "Like there's a whole other layer just out of sight. The evidence makes sense, but it's not the whole story."

His case notes from 2024 reflected this growing awareness. During the River District Disappearances, he wrote: "Victims vanish on full moons. The standard missing persons protocol feels inadequate. Something primal about these cases." By 2025, investigating the Warehouse District Murders, his observations grew sharper: "Blood spatter patterns defy physics. Medical examiner's reports contain inconsistencies they can't explain. Getting that feeling again."

The PAC's reforms created specialized units like the Digital Shadow Team, composed of tech-savvy pack members who maintained pack security in the digital age. They monitored social media for potential exposure, created convincing digital histories, and scrubbed supernatural indicators from surveillance systems.

The Human Interface Protocol became mandatory training for pack members in professional positions. They learned sophisticated methods for managing medical records to hide supernatural healing, explaining enhanced physical capabilities, and maintaining consistent human identities under scrutiny.

Masters' growing intuition led to his unofficial designation as a "Threshold Officer" - someone who could work supernatural cases without full knowledge. Pack security actually incorporated his investigative instincts into their protocols, establishing that when Detective Masters expressed concerns about a case's unusual elements, immediate review was required.

The Walsh case had exposed critical vulnerabilities. Modern surveillance made traditional territory patterns detectable, digital records could reveal supernatural inconsistencies, and scientific analysis could identify supernatural characteristics. Rather than fight these challenges, the new measures adapted to them. Pack meetings now rotated locations using algorithm-generated patterns. Medical records were systematically managed through a network of aware or threshold medical professionals. Scientific anomalies were masked by deliberately introduced false data patterns.

The PAC's reforms included detailed contingency plans for exposure scenarios, ranging from individual incidents to mass exposure risks. Each level triggered specific responses, from containment through official channels to full pack mobilization with predetermined evacuation routes and cover identities.

Masters' role evolved to become an unofficial bridge between worlds. His investigations often paralleled supernatural incidents, his conventional police work inadvertently supporting pack security. The Walsh Protocols proved their worth during subsequent incidents, like the Stadium Incident of 2024, where a werewolf transformation during a crowded sports event was successfully contained through predetermined media management and evidence control protocols.

His partnership with Ethan deepened, built on unspoken understanding. "Some things don't need full explanations," he noted after a particularly unusual case.

"Sometimes it's enough to know justice was served, even if we don't understand exactly how."

The Pack Killer case had initiated a new era in supernatural security. The Walsh Protocols transformed pack operations from simple secrecy to sophisticated security management. Masters's evolving role demonstrated the potential for human-supernatural cooperation, even without full disclosure.

Ethan's position as bridge between worlds gained new significance. He helped refine the protocols based on practical experience, balancing supernatural security with effective law enforcement. His reports to both human and supernatural authorities became templates for future cases.

The supernatural community learned vital lessons about modern survival. Secrecy alone was no longer sufficient protection. The new protocols acknowledged the need for active security management in an increasingly connected world.

Masters never learned the full truth, but his intuitive understanding proved invaluable. His cases became case studies in successful threshold operations - how to achieve justice across worlds without compromising either. The Pack Killer's legacy wasn't just enhanced security - it was a new understanding of how supernatural communities could adapt to modern scrutiny while maintaining their essential secrets. Each new case tested and refined these protocols, preparing for a future where the line between worlds grew increasingly thin.

CHAPTER TWENTY-FIVE

CHANGING PARTNERS

MASTERS DELIVERED the news over coffee at their usual corner shop. "Federal task force. Organized crime division." He pushed the official letter across the table. "They want me to start next month."

Ethan nodded, masking his unease behind the congratulations. Seven years of partnership had created a delicate balance. Masters' intuitive grasp of when to stop asking questions, when to accept unconventional explanations, had become fundamental to Ethan's dual existence.

"You deserve it," Ethan said, meaning it despite his concerns. Masters had solved impossible cases, though he'd never known exactly how impossible they truly were. His case closure rate was exceptional, even if his reports sometimes contained careful omissions that only Ethan understood.

Later, reviewing their years together, Ethan cataloged the close calls. The warehouse raid where Masters had glimpsed Ethan's eyes reflecting unnaturally in darkness, but attributed it to tactical lighting. The chase where supernatural speed had been explained away as adrenaline and good timing. Countless crime scenes where Masters's growing intuition had approached supernatural awareness without quite crossing that line.

Amber visited his apartment that evening, bringing case files and concern. "I heard about Masters's promotion. The Council is worried about transition risks."

The Council had reason for concern. Masters' threshold awareness - his ability to work supernatural cases without full knowledge - had developed organically over years. His replacement would arrive without that carefully cultivated understanding.

"They're assigning Alice Chen," Amber said, spreading personnel files across Ethan's kitchen table."Top of her class at Quantico. Three years with Chicago Homicide. Impressive solve rate."

The file painted a picture of methodical brilliance. Chen specialized in pattern recognition, finding connections others missed. Her case notes showed relentless attention to detail. No anomaly too small to investigate, no inconsistency left unexplained.

"She could be problematic," Amber noted. "That level of scrutiny..."

Ethan studied Chen's photograph. Sharp eyes, slight smile. Her case histories showed a preference for unconventional theories when evidence warranted. She'd solved a series of apparent suicides by proving they were elaborate murders, tracking subtle patterns others had dismissed.

"Or she could be perfect," Ethan countered. "Someone who can accept unusual explanations when facts support them."

Masters' last week brought a parade of farewell gestures. The department gave him a plaque. Fellow officers shared drinks and stories. Only Ethan understood the true significance of some cases they reminisced about.

"Something I never told you," Masters said during their final case review. "Half the time, I knew your explanations weren't complete. Didn't need them to be. Results mattered more than methods."

The admission stunned Ethan. "How long?"

"Remember the Riverside murders? You explained away the weird blood patterns with some complicated theory about angle of impact. I knew it was wrong, but I also knew you had good reasons for the cover story. Figured if you needed me to know more, you'd tell me."

Their last morning as partners, Masters handed Ethan an envelope. "My private notes on our cases. Things that never made it into official reports. Might help you with the next partner."

Reading them later, Ethan discovered Masters had seen more than anyone realized. His unofficial observations noted patterns in lunar cycles, references to strange scents and sounds, unexplained healing. He'd recorded everything but drawn no conclusions, maintaining plausible deniability while preserving crucial details.

Alice Chen arrived the following Monday, her precision evident in everything from her pressed suit to her organized approach to introductions. "Detective Chen," she said, handshake firm. "I've studied your case histories. You have unusual methods, but impressive results."

Her desk setup revealed her nature: multiple monitors for data analysis, case files arranged by pattern rather than chronology, a wall space soon filled with interconnected theories and timelines.

"I believe in following evidence wherever it leads," she explained, arranging her systems."Even when the destination seems impossible."

That first week tested Ethan's adaptability. Chen analyzed everything, building complex theoretical frameworks around each case element. Her questions were precise, targeted, designed to expose inconsistencies in conventional explanations.

"The blood spatter in the Russel case," she noted on day three. "The official report suggests standard arterial spray, but the pattern indicates impossible directionality. Thoughts?"

Ethan felt the familiar tension between truth and secrecy. With Masters, he'd learned to navigate these moments through years of partnership. Chen's analytical mind demanded more immediate solutions.

Amber provided unexpected insight during their weekly council meeting. "She's not Masters, and we shouldn't want her to be. His strength was knowing when not to ask questions. Hers might be asking exactly the right ones."

The supernatural community adjusted their protocols. Chen's pattern recognition skills meant tighter control on evidence management. Her digital expertise required more sophisticated cover story coordination. Every case needed deeper preparation, more careful execution.

"Your new partner," Alpha Regina observed, "might force us to improve our methods. Sometimes pressure creates necessary change."

Ethan began developing new approaches to bridging his worlds. Where Masters's threshold awareness had evolved naturally, Chen's potential required careful cultivation. Her analytical mind might accept supernatural reality if presented through logical progression.

The transition marked more than a simple partner change. It represented evolution in the delicate balance between human and supernatural worlds. Masters's promotion closed one chapter in this ongoing adaptation, while Chen's arrival opened new possibilities.

"Change is inevitable," Amber reminded him. "The question is whether we let it weaken us or make us stronger."

As Ethan filed Masters' private notes in his supernatural case archive, he reflected on the cycles of change. Each transition carried risks and opportunities. Masters' intuitive acceptance had allowed one kind of bridge between worlds. Perhaps Chen's analytical brilliance would forge another.

The future remained uncertain, but uncertainty had always been part of straddling two worlds. As Ethan prepared for his first solo case with Chen, he recognized the familiar challenge: maintaining necessary secrets while pursuing justice across the boundaries of natural and supernatural law.

Masters' last text arrived that evening: "Sometimes the best partners are the ones who help us grow in unexpected ways."

Looking at Chen's elaborate case analysis spreading across her desk, Ethan understood that adaptation wasn't just about maintaining secrets - it was about finding new ways to reveal the truth without compromising either world. The next chapter was beginning, and its shape would depend on how well he could balance change with continuity, revelation with protection, and the ever-shifting line between known and unknown.

EPILOGUE: BETWEEN WORLDS

One year after the Pack Killer case, Ethan stood at his window overlooking the city lights, a collection of case files spread across his desk. The Walsh Protocols had transformed supernatural security, but they'd also changed him. Each case now carried the weight of two worlds' expectations - the human need for justice and the supernatural requirement for secrecy.

The city had evolved too. Amber's efforts had strengthened the networks between various supernatural communities. The werewolf packs operated with newfound sophistication, their ancient hierarchies adapting to modern challenges. Even the threshold network - those humans who worked supernatural cases without full knowledge - had grown more refined in their approach.

His phone buzzed with a text from Masters: "Federal task force investigating tech company. CEO's blood work shows impossible results. Thinking of you."

The message highlighted how far they'd come. Masters' new position occasionally intersected with supernatural cases, and he'd maintained his careful balance of awareness and discretion. His unofficial reports still found their way to Ethan's desk, marked with the subtle indicators they'd developed over years of partnership.

Amber's voice mail followed: "Council meeting tomorrow. New patterns emerging in the wake of Walsh. Some think we're approaching a tipping point."

The Walsh case had exposed vulnerabilities, but it had also revealed strengths. The supernatural community's ability to adapt, to find new ways of hiding in plain sight, proved more resilient than anyone expected. Modern surveillance created challenges, but it also provided opportunities for misdirection and coverage.

Ethan's role had evolved beyond simple detective work. He'd become a crucial bridge between worlds, helping shape policies that protected supernatural secrets while serving human justice. His case files now contained two versions of every story - the official reports for human authorities and the true accounts for supernatural records.

The city spread before him, its lights concealing countless secrets. Somewhere out there, werewolves ran their territory under the cover of routine patrols. Threshold doctors treated supernatural injuries in quiet hospital rooms. Pack members maintained their human lives while protecting ancient traditions.

His phone lit up again - a priority alert from dispatch. Three bodies discovered in the warehouse district, showing signs of unusual trauma. The preliminary reports included terms that triggered supernatural protocols: unexplained healing, anomalous tissue damage, temporal inconsistencies.

As Ethan gathered his coat and badge, he reflected on the delicate balance he maintained. Every case was a chance to protect both worlds, to serve justice while preserving necessary secrets. The challenge wasn't getting easier, but he was getting better at meeting it.

The city needed both versions of him - the human detective who solved impossible cases and the supernatural guardian who kept ancient secrets. As he headed out into the night, Ethan knew that each case brought them closer to a future where those roles might become harder to separate.

But that was tomorrow's challenge. Tonight, there were bodies in the warehouse district, and both his worlds needed answers. As always, he would find a way to serve them both, walking the ever-thinning line between what was known and what had to remain hidden.

The game of secrets and shadows continued, evolving with each new case, each new challenge. And Ethan, standing between worlds, would keep playing his part in maintaining that crucial balance - one case, one secret, one justice at a time.

A SNEAK PEEK AT WHAT'S NEXT!

THANK you for joining me on this journey through **Moonlight Origins: The Making of a Werewolf Detective.** I hope you enjoyed exploring the mysteries of Daybridge and getting to know its secrets.

The story doesn't end here—there's so much more waiting to be uncovered. I'm excited to give you an exclusive first look at **Shadows Between Thoughts,** the next book in the *Ethan Reeves Werewolf Detective Series.* Dive into the free chapter below and get a taste of what's to come!

Prologue: Echoes in the Darkness

The abandoned halls of Daybridge Maximum Security Hospital whispered with the weight of its dark history. Once a beacon of healing, the sprawling gothic structure now stood as a decaying reminder of the unspeakable acts that had taken place within its walls.

For Ryan Matthews, Jojo Lang, and Jason Reeves, the allure of uncovering the hospital's secrets had been too powerful to resist. As professional ghost hunters, they had ventured into the building's shadowy depths, armed with cameras, voice recorders, and an insatiable curiosity for the paranormal. Little did they know that their investigation would awaken a malevolent force that had lain dormant for decades.

On that fateful night, the ghost hunters had made their way through the twisting corridors, their flashlights casting eerie shadows on the peeling walls. The air grew colder with each step, and a sense of unease crept over them like a suffocating blanket.

In a dimly lit room that had once served as a doctor's office, they discovered a trove of patient files and medical journals. The musty papers held dark secrets, hinting at unethical experiments and twisted practices carried out in the name of science. As they delved deeper into the disturbing records, a sudden gust of icy wind extinguished their lights, plunging them into darkness.

Disembodied whispers filled the room, growing louder and more urgent with each passing second. The ghost hunters froze, their hearts pounding in their chests as an invisible presence seemingly surrounded them. Ryan, the leader of the group, tried to rationalize the experience, but deep down, he knew they had stumbled upon something far more sinister than a simple haunting.

Jason, driven by an inexplicable urge, reached out to touch one of the old medical devices. As his fingers brushed against the cold metal, a jolt of energy surged through his body, and visions of unspeakable horrors flooded his mind. He saw patients strapped to gurneys, their screams echoing through the halls as a shadowy figure loomed over them, wielding glinting surgical tools.

Jojo, the tech expert, frantically tried to capture the paranormal activity on her modified camera, but the device malfunctioned, its screen flickering with distorted images of twisted faces and ghostly apparitions. The very walls seemed to pulse with a malevolent energy, as if the hospital itself was alive and angry at their intrusion.

Overwhelmed by the intensity of the encounter, the ghost hunters fled, their footsteps echoing through the abandoned corridors. But as they raced toward the exit, a sinister force took hold, determined to keep them within its grasp. Doors slammed shut, trapping them in a labyrinth of darkness, and an unearthly howl reverberated through the building, shaking them to their core.

From that moment on, Ryan, Jojo, and Jason were never seen again. Or were they? Their disappearance sparked whispers of the hospital's curse and tales of the vengeful spirits that roamed its halls. The ghost hunters' families were left with unanswered questions and a growing sense of dread, desperate for any clue that might lead to their loved ones' whereabouts.

Now, two weeks after their vanishing, the case has landed on the desk of Ethan Reeves, a seasoned detective with a secret of his own. As a werewolf, Ethan possesses heightened senses and supernatural abilities that have served him well in his investigations. Alongside his trusted partner, Alice, he must venture into the depths of Daybridge Hospital and confront the malevolent forces that lurk within.

But as Ethan delves deeper into the mystery, he realizes that the disappearance of the ghost hunters is just the beginning. A twisted web of secrets, born from the hospital's dark past, threatens to ensnare them all. With time running out and the shadows closing in, Ethan must use all his skills and cunning to unravel the truth, save the missing ghost hunters, and confront the evil that stalks the halls of Daybridge hospital.

For in the abandoned wards and hidden laboratories, something wicked has awakened, hungry for vengeance and ready to unleash its fury upon the world. And only Ethan Reeves stands between the darkness and the unsuspecting souls beyond the hospital's cursed walls.

～

ABOUT THE AUTHOR

Rae Stonehouse turned to fiction writing after establishing himself as a prolific author of self-development and professional growth books.

With over 50 published works helping readers navigate personal and professional challenges, he embarked on a new creative path with the Ethan Reeves Werewolf Detective Series.

When not weaving tales of supernatural sleuthing, Stonehouse continues to share his expertise in personal development through workshops and speaking engagements from his home in British Columbia.

The Ethan Reeves series marks his debut in fiction writing, blending his understanding of human nature with a newfound passion for urban fantasy.

www.ingramcontent.com/pod-product-compliance
Lightning Source LLC
Chambersburg PA
CBHW061354310726
48974CB00001B/336